The Cha

Gill Arbuthnott

The Chaos Clock

Kelpies

Kelpies is an imprint of Floris Books

First published in Kelpies in 2003
Published in 2003 by Floris Books
Reprinted 2004

The publisher acknowledges a Lottery grant
from the Scottish Arts Council towards the
publication of this series.

British Library CIP Data available

ISBN 0–86315–422-0

Printed in Europe

For my mother and father
who taught me to love stories
and for Tom
who never reads them

Contents

Prologue

The rising wind howled through the small trees at the water's edge, flattening the grass between the village and the loch.

"Hurry. We don't have much time."

The Smith took no notice.

"The blade will not be hurried." He raised the hammer and brought it down once more on the edge of the sword he was forging. "Are the children away?"

"Yes. The village is empty save for us four. Listen."

Twisted into the noise of the wind were other sounds: voices, howling, roars, grinding.

The Chief caught the Smith's arm as he raised it again. "There is no more time. Quench the blade."

The Smith nodded shortly. "Go. Stand with the others. I will bring the sword." He raised it from the great, blackened oak stump that served as an anvil and, his hand protected by thick layers of leather, dropped it into the tub of water. The water boiled as it cooled the metal and the air filled with the reek of hot bronze. Satisfied, the Chief lifted the deerskin, which served as a door curtain.

Outside in the twilight, two women waited: the Wise Woman and the Smith's wife. They stood braced against the wind, looking around for the source of the howls and cries that it carried to them.

The Wise Woman handed the Chief a spear, bronze-headed with a shaft of rowan wood. In her right hand she held a bronze dagger with a hilt of polished bone. The Smith's wife had a throwing-axe, also of bronze, jet-handled.

"Where is the sword?" The Wise Woman shouted over the chaos of noise.

"In the quenching tub. A few more seconds ..."

The loch in front of them began to seethe. The Smith's wife gasped and gripped the axe harder. Thunder growled behind the hill.

The Smith came out of the hut carrying the sword, with its deerskin grip and the piece of gold set into the pommel, as the storm broke over them.

Sheets of water so heavy it could scarcely be called rain beat at them, flattening the grass around them and bending the trees. Lightning cracked the darkening sky and thunder roared and growled.

Out of the storm rode the Lords of Chaos — beasts, horned and fanged, human forms and some figures that were both or neither. At their head were the Great Ones: the Queen of Darkness, crowned with stars, on a night-black horse whose eyes burned like coals; the Water Witch, rain pouring from her uplifted hands; the Hunter, horned and owl-eyed, daubed with blood; and the Lightning King, gaunt and dark, his robes whipping in the wind, blue eyes blazing, lightning splitting the air around him.

The four villagers drew closer together, impossibly fragile in the face of the onslaught of Chaos.

"Not yet," called the Chief. "They must be closer."

Without looking around, he held out his hand to the Smith.

"Give me the sword. Take the spear, throw when I tell you."

"No."

"Yes. The sword is for me to use. Take the spear." He turned to look at the Smith. "You cannot play my part in this battle."

The Smith smiled. "I know what your part is to be. The sword is of my forging. I will use it."

"Fool! I must pay the price, not you."

"Quickly! They are upon us." The Wise Woman shouted to be heard over the storm, and then, truly, there was no more time. The Chief and the Wise Woman began to chant and suddenly the weapons blazed with golden light.

Far beyond the other side of the loch, the rest of the village watched the golden light battle the darkness and lightning across the sky, and the Smith's children waited fearfully for their parents.

For the best part of an hour they watched, as the light and dark waxed and waned and the thunder roared over the hill, then, as suddenly as it had begun, the storm ceased and the lights died away, and the stars shone as they should.

And the people waited.

The empty village was silent. Outside the forge were four people, the weapons in their hands bent and broken and blackened. Of the Lords of Chaos there was no sign. The Smith lay still and flat on the ground, the remains of the sword by his side. The others knelt by him.

"Was it enough?" he asked with an obvious effort.

His wife answered. "It was enough. They are gone and the village is safe."

He spoke then to the Chief, turning his head a little to see him.

"You are needed more than I am. I am a willing sacrifice." He was silent for some seconds then added, "It was a good sword."

He did not speak again.

When his body had been burned with due ceremony and the mourning feast was over, they took the broken weapons and the oak bole down to the water's edge, at a place where the loch bed dropped sharply away. All the villagers watched as the Smith's children threw the weapons into the shining water. Then two of the young men heaved the anvil stump in after them.

"It is finished," said the Chief. "For this time we are safe. The willing sacrifice has been made. Go to your own hearths and give thanks."

As the people drifted away the Chief and the Wise Woman were left alone on the shore.

"Why the anvil too?" she asked him.

"The power of the forging passed into it as well as into the weapons. It too must pass from our world. The power can be used for ill as readily as for good." He sighed, his milky blue gaze on the embers of the Smith's pyre. "It should not have been him. I have known since the day that the hunters came back to the village and told us they had seen four spirits on the other side of the loch that Chaos was rising and that the battle was drawing near. I was ready."

"But you said to the villagers — he was the willing sacrifice."

"But the wrong one! It should have been me who died. I do not know what will come of this ..."

1. The Clock

The first time she found one of the little handprints, Mary Sinclair didn't think much about it. She knew it wasn't a child's hand — it was too narrow, the fingers too long — so she assumed it must be from a toy; a very detailed toy, to be sure, for you could see the imprint of the lines on the palm and at the knuckles, that had been pressed against the glass as its owner let it look at the wolves, running through the trees.

She squirted it with glass cleaner, polished it away and forgot about it.

"Come on Mum, we're going to be late." Kate Dalgliesh stood by the front door, shifting impatiently from foot to foot and twirling a strand of blonde hair between her fingers.

"All right, all right, I'm coming. Where are the car keys?"

Kate rolled her eyes. "They're here by the front door. I told you already."

"I've just got to get Ben's shoes on." Her mother's voice sounded muffled, as though her head was in a wardrobe.

It probably was, Kate thought. "They're here too," she called.

"Oh. Okay."

Ben came rushing round the corner, a toy plane clutched in one hand, making death-to-all-earthlings noises, closely followed by Ruth, Kate's mother. She wrestled him into his shoes and picked up the car keys she had carefully filed on the floor by the front door so she couldn't lose them.

"Ready?"

"Mum, I've been standing here for ten minutes."

"Two," said Ruth.

Kate grinned. "Five."

"Okay, five. Now let's go. David will think you've forgotten."

The monkey wore a golden hat, collar and skirt. There was a bell on her tail and bracelets of gold on her arms. She held a handle, which looked as if it should turn an enormous wheel of rusty looking metal, linked in its turn to others. From behind the assembly of cogs and gears peered out a great bearded man, hung about with chains.

David stared and stared and stared, brown eyes wide.

"Well, what do you think?"

He'd been so absorbed that Kate's voice coming from behind him made him jump, and when he turned to her, it was with a look of baffled delight on his face.

"It's incredible. How long has it been here?"

"Since the New Year. It's called the Millennium Clock."

They both craned their necks upward looking at the top of the clock, almost two storeys above them.

"It's like a rocket, or a church spire or something."

"Wait 'til you hear it."

"Does it chime?"

"Nothing as boring as that. Just wait. We'll come back at three."

David dragged his gaze away, pushing his dark hair out of his eyes. "I suppose we'd better go and start this project. What time's your mum coming?"

"Ben's show finishes at half past three, so just after that."

They picked up their rucksacks and wandered away from the clock, talking, past the two rows of chairs with their high linked backs that looked like a whale's rib bones.

On one of them sat a white-haired old man in a checked jacket, who watched them from milky blue eyes. There was an open sketch pad on his knees, with a half-done drawing of the clock. Immersed in talk, they passed him unaware, but he turned slowly to watch them until they were lost in a group at the doorway to the new part of the museum.

Kate and David had a lot of talking to catch up on. David had only been back from Houston for three weeks and they'd been apart for a whole year. They'd talked on the phone of course during that time and written and emailed each other, but it wasn't the same as being together and just talking. Neither of them had realized quite how much they'd missed each other until David came back and they started again.

Neither of them could remember a time before they'd been friends. They'd been together since they were just a few months old, starting nursery together.

They'd stayed friends all the way up primary school and even David's time in Houston — where his father, who worked for one of the oil companies, had been sent for a year — didn't seem to have changed anything.

They headed down the wooden steps towards the bottom floor of the New Museum (officially the Museum of Scotland, but they never called it that), where the oldest things were, the ones that would help them with "Scotland's Early People." Jamie Grieve, the self-appointed class clown, had said did that mean postmen and newsagents, and Mrs Henderson had looked at him, not very amused, while the rest of the class laughed much too loudly for such a feeble joke.

"Let's go and look at the animals before we start," said David, and they turned into the gallery with the long diorama of the animals that used to roam Scotland before people did: bear and wild pig, a beaver suspended mid-splash, wolves howling among the trees and the little lemming tucked up warmly beneath the snow.

David peered around the edge of the winter scene into the corner and gave a yelp of pleasure. "It's still there. I thought somebody with no sense of humour would have taken it away by now."

He'd been looking at a little snowman, hidden away where you'd not see it unless you knew where to look.

They made their way between display cases to the screens that showed how the Iron Age people built their houses and settlements, and watched the whole sequence three times, sitting in silence on the dusty seat, writing and drawing.

David glanced at his watch. "It's ten to three. I want to hear the clock striking — or whatever it does."

They gathered their things and went back up through the layers of time to the ground floor.

Around the clock, a small crowd had already gathered as though waiting for it to explode out of the glass roof like a firework. As the hands reached the hour, the clock came to life.

First, music, as though an invisible church organ hung in the air. The monkey began to turn her handle and all the wheels and gears in the lowest section started to move. Bathed in red and blue light, the great chained figure behind her looked out from his prison.

Abruptly, the monkey stopped and the middle section of the clock took up the story with bells and wind chimes and grotesque automata bobbing and whirling; and the great convex-mirrored pendulum, a skeleton sitting on top of it, swung slowly, slowly, reflecting the distorted faces of its audience.

Deeper bells sounded now, tolling, not chiming and a circle of figures high above David's head began to revolve. They were so high that he hadn't looked at them closely before, but now he saw that they showed people suffering, in pain and frightened. He made out a figure swathed in barbed wire and another with a Star of David round its neck.

The whole clock was in motion now, the monkey turning her handle, the donkeys shaking the bells in their mouths, red light glowing at the top of the spire.

The monkey stopped again, then the music. The lights died and the whole mechanism gradually came to rest, the last sound the sweet notes of the wind chimes.

When even that had died away, everyone who had been watching and listening was still for a few seconds.

David turned to Kate. "It's amazing. What's it about? It's like a story, but I don't know what it is." He was walking around the base of the clock as he spoke, squinting up to the top of the spire, where the donkeys with the bells in their mouths looked out.

"Let's go upstairs. You can see more of it from there," suggested Kate, blue eyes shining.

As they started up the steps they heard their names being called and turned to see Ruth and Ben coming towards them.

"You're early, Mum."

"We came out at the interval. It was too noisy even for Ben, if you can believe that, and they'd have had to take me out in a straightjacket if we'd stayed until the end. I've promised Ben a drink. Do you want to come, or are you too busy with your project?"

"We've got time for a break," said David quickly.

"Come on then."

They turned away from the stairs to head for the café.

"Ruth, my dear. How good to see you."

"Mr Flowerdew! How are you?"

It was the old man with the sketch pad.

"Very well thank you. And you and the family?"

"We're fine," said Ruth, trying to restrain Ben, who was pulling on her arm, anxious for a can of juice. "Ben's four and a half now and Kate's just turned eleven. So has David, of course. You remember David Fairbairn?"

"David, of course. Still like drawing?"

He smiled and nodded, suddenly shy but pleased to have been remembered. Mr Flowerdew had been a friend of Kate's Grandma Alice. David had met him a few times when Grandma Alice looked after Kate and him as she sometimes did when they were small. Mr Flowerdew used to draw for him — dinosaurs and dragons and soldiers mostly — and help him with his own pictures. He'd not seen him since Grandma Alice died when they were eight, but he looked just the same, even the jacket.

"We were just going to the café," Ruth was saying. "Come and have a cup of tea. It's too long since we've seen you."

Mr Flowerdew pulled out an old-fashioned pocket watch. "I would love to, my dear, but unfortunately I have to be somewhere else in half an hour. Another time though."

He shifted his gaze to the children. "I'm often here sketching. Come and find me next time you're here to do your project and I'll take you for an ice cream." He put the watch back in his pocket. "I must be on my way. We'll see each other soon. Goodbye." He walked off towards the revolving door, waving over his shoulder as he went.

After they'd had their drinks, as they hurried to get to the car before the parking ticket ran out, David asked Kate the question that had been nagging at him. "How did he know we were doing a project?"

"What?"

"Mr Flowerdew. How did he know we were here to work on our project?"

Kate frowned, trying to remember how the conversation had gone.

"We didn't tell him and neither did your mum."

"And Mrs Henderson only set the project last week and it's ages since I've seen him."

They thought hard as they went around the revolving door.

"He must just have guessed when he saw me carrying a folder," said Kate, but she didn't sound convinced.

On the pavement at the bottom of the stairs a small dog sat, looking up expectantly at the museum, as though waiting for someone to come out.

"Mummy, I want to pat the doggie," Ben was saying.

"Oh, all right. He looks friendly enough."

He was some sort of little rough-coated terrier, a Skye or a Border maybe. They all had a turn of scratching him behind the ears and under the chin, his bedraggled plume of a tail thumping on the pavement with pleasure.

"I wonder who he belongs to? He's not wearing a collar," said David.

"He wasn't here when we arrived," said Kate, "was he, Mum?"

"Well, I don't remember seeing him," said Ruth.

"Anyway, we must go now. I'm sure he'll be fine. Say goodbye to the doggie, Ben."

They got to the car just before a traffic warden. As they drove off, Kate and David looked back, to where the little dog sat, patiently waiting.

That night, David dreamed that he was standing on a beach of small pebbles. Before him lay an enormous lake, stretching into a distance lost in mist. Not a ripple disturbed its surface. It lay heavily and flatly silver like a pool of mercury.

In the dream, he'd been standing there for a long time, staring forward into nothing, afraid to turn his head, when from the corner of his eye, he saw something move on his right and automatically turned sharply to look at it.

He woke with a start, breathing hard and sat up, fumbling for his bedside lamp. Yellow light filled the room, familiar objects all around him. He listened to his heart slow to its normal pace, shivering. The room was cold and David realized he'd forgotten to shut the window. Pushing aside the curtains to reach for the sash, he saw that it was misty outside, the street lamp an uncertain wavering glow instead of the usual clear yellow halo beyond the garden. He shut the window firmly and tugged the curtains together. Before he climbed back into bed he looked at his alarm clock. Quarter past two. He pulled the covers round his ears and shut his eyes.

2. *A Quiet Night*

Gordon Syme was bored. He didn't like doing the night shift. Some of his colleagues looked forward to it; money for nothing, they said. You could soon find a comfy wee corner and as long as you took a bit of a wander every so often there was no problem. There were alarms on all the really valuable stuff and a proper security man watching the pictures from the security cameras, and after all, nobody was likely to break in and steal one of the elephants now, were they?

Trouble was, Gordon couldn't do things that way. His conscience wouldn't let him nap the night away, or maybe he was just too tall for the wee cubby holes so many of the others seemed to find.

So here he was, ten o'clock at night, leafing through the diary at the Information Desk to see if anything interesting was coming up in the next few weeks, trying to pretend that he wasn't going to be stuck in here all boring night long.

There was a crew from some Arts programme coming in to film the clock on Wednesday afternoon. That might be good for a laugh, though they'd probably want everyone kept back out of the way and he'd have to spend the whole afternoon stopping people from going where they wanted.

Looking further ahead, he saw there was going to be another sleepover in two weeks time. Now that was one time he did like doing night shift. Kids in sleeping bags all over the place and precious little sleep. You'd to keep them from choosing a place to bed down that was too spooky mind you: chase them out from where the mummies waited, bandaged, for paradise, for example. Another place they'd stopped using was the gallery above the dinosaurs, the one with the elk and the ground sloth skeletons. There was something creepy about that place in the dead of night. None of the attendants ever kipped there, in spite of the padded benches.

The shark display was popular with sleepover kids. Apart from the attraction of the sharks themselves, there was the rippling light that washed over the area, like sun seen through waves. It was a good place to get sleepy.

There was a creaking rattle from the far end of the Hall. Gordon looked up sharply and caught a faint gleam from the clock-monkey's golden collar in the dim light, as she turned her handle and the whole extraordinary edifice began to move in near silence. The music was switched off when the museum closed for the night, but you couldn't turn a clockwork mechanism that size on and off so easily, so it went through the whole show without accompaniment.

Gordon found it even more unsettling without the music. Its own bells were chiming now, the tortured figures near the top circling slowly, a clink from the whirling chains of the skeleton as the donkey heads shook the bells in their mouths. The thing was only supposed to have been here for three months, but the arrangements for wherever it had been supposed to go next had fallen through, so here it was for the foreseeable future.

Ah well, time to go for a stroll. Gordon picked up his torch and looked at his watch. Five past ten. Oh no …

Gordon looked at his watch. Two o'clock. "Better take a wander then, Sandy," he said, draining his mug.

"Aye, right enough," said Sandy, making no move to get up.

"Come on then."

With a theatrical sigh, Sandy rose and followed Gordon out from the staff tearoom and down to the bottom floor of the new part of the museum.

They walked together as far as the metal men, then separated. This was an old routine and each knew without question which parts of the galleries were his responsibility.

Gordon headed for the lowest room that was ever open to the public: the round chamber that held the carved Pictish stones, with their engraved animals and geometric patterns.

The air-conditioning was a constant hum in the background, like half-heard whispers, and as he looked around Gordon was acutely aware of the seven museum floors above him, a sense of their weight pressing down on his head.

As he left the room, the swinging torch beam caught an ancient wooden figure, with stones for eyes, imprisoned in a cage of oak twigs near the doorway. He walked up the sloping passage from the round room and felt her stony gaze in the small of his back, and made an effort not to quicken his pace.

In the central area of this level, life-sized metal men were caught in the act of marching or standing or sitting. They were blocky figures, half robotic but with rib cages and unexpectedly human hands and faces. Set into the figures in various places were little glass cases holding jewellery of gold and silver, bronze and jet, amber and bone: all powerful things from olden times.

Walking briskly Gordon turned into the room where, frozen in time, animals loped, flew and crawled through a Scotland that had disappeared thousands of years ago. How far did he walk during a night shift, he wondered? It always felt further than during the day.

When he had finished there, he went into the biggest of the display areas on this level to meet up with Sandy. He could see Sandy's torch beam moving among the cases at the far side of the gallery near a wall of cracked red clay with a snake shape twisting down it.

He caught his breath. What was that?

He spun round, eyes wide, skin prickling, breath caught. From the corner of his eye he'd seen something move down on the floor, flicking round the corner of a case.

He aimed his light at the spot, but there was nothing. "Sandy, come here," he called, his voice sounding strange even to himself, and heard hurried footsteps in response.

"What is it, man?"

"I saw something go round that case. A rat maybe, or a cat that's got in somehow."

"Are you sure?" Sandy went round the case, sweeping the beam of his torch around.

"It was just a glimpse, but there was definitely something. We'd better put the lights on, have a proper look."

He went to where the switches were, trying to lose the prickling sensation running down his spine, and put all the lights on. Sandy was crouched down looking between cases for any sign of what Gordon had seen. Gordon himself didn't think it would have been likely to stay in the same place and walked to the far end of the big room.

Once, a few years ago now, they'd found a rat like this and a couple of times a cat had sneaked in. Pest control came round regularly now, so he didn't imagine that this had been a rat. It had been much too big for a rat anyway, nor had it looked like a cat, though he'd only had a glimpse.

It must have been a cat.

He still couldn't shake off the feeling that all his hair was standing up. He and Sandy checked the gallery from end to end, but there was no sign of whatever it was that Gordon had seen. He looked at his watch. Quarter past two. It was turning into a long night.

3. The Cold Desert

"Kate!"

Kate was jolted back to the here and now with a sensation as though she'd hit the ground from a great height.

"Yes, Mrs Henderson?"

"You were miles away there. Pay attention, please."

Kate shifted in her seat, and took a deep breath to try and shake off the half-asleep feeling that had dogged her since lunch time. She'd been daydreaming about Grandma Alice just now, even though it was nearly three years since she'd died. She felt a bit guilty that she didn't think about her more often. They'd been special to each other; Kate had known since she was very small that she was the favourite grandchild, although Grandma Alice had never treated her any differently from the other three. She'd even treated David as a sort of grandson. It was only when she died and left Kate the gold necklace that she singled her out.

There she went, back into a daydream again. She sat up extra straight and tried to concentrate on Maths. The sun didn't make it any easier of course, reflecting off the frosted glass of the windows to her right and throwing dazzling multi-coloured snowflakes across her field of vision.

Kate looked at Mrs Henderson, doing her best to listen, but although the teacher's mouth was moving, no sounds came out. Instead, behind her, there was a noise like the sea rolling in across sand. She turned through the dazzle of snowflakes to see where the noise could be coming from. For a few seconds everything was blindingly white and then …

She stood in a wasteland of blowing sand, cold and alone. When she turned round it stretched beyond the limits of her vision in every direction. Faintly, on the edge of hearing, was the sound of something howling. The noise made her shiver. She kept turning slowly, straining to see something other than the endless plain of sand.

There was a figure. But where had it come from? It hadn't been there a few seconds ago. Against the sun's glare reflected off the sand, Kate could make it out only as someone walking towards her.

Now it was a woman wearing a long dress. How had she come so near so quickly? Three metres from Kate the woman stopped and stood silent, her dark green dress clinging wetly to her. Her long brown hair was wet too, darkened by moisture. Greenish water trickled without pause from her hair, hands and dress onto the sand and disappeared.

She smiled, her mouth pomegranate-red, and held out a hand. "Kate, my dear."

Her voice was low and rich. Mesmerized, Kate watched the water drip from her long, pale fingers.

"Who are you?"

"My name does not matter for now." She moved forward slowly, her arm still outstretched. Her eyes were the colour of smoke. Her red lips smiled. In the distance the faint howling continued.

She moved forwards. "It is time for us to meet. We have been waiting for so long ..."

Kate moved one slow step away. "Who's been waiting? How do you know my name?"

Smiling mouth, smoky eyes, trickle of water. Outstretched hand.

"Shhh."

A finger touched her forehead. Cold. Water trickled into her eyes, clouding her lashes. She blinked, trying to look through it and saw a dazzle of snowflakes.

"Kate?"

She put her hand up to wipe the water from her eyes, to push the cold fingers away from her.

"It's all right, Kate."

She opened her eyes. Mrs Henderson was looking at her, frowning. Mrs Henderson was looking *down* at her. She seemed to be lying on the floor.

She sat up, confusion and embarrassment fighting for space in her head.

"Take your time, Kate. How do you feel?"

Looking round now, she saw faces turned towards her, eyes wide, David among them, his forehead furrowed in a frown.

"I feel fine. I'm all right." It was true. She did feel fine. She felt stupid.

"What happened?"

"You fainted, dear. Just for a few seconds. Nothing to worry about, it happens to lots of people. I sent someone for the nurse."

Kate got to her feet, Mrs Henderson insisting on helping, and sat down on her chair, so embarrassed she wished she could disappear. She knew her face must be scarlet and she tried without success to ignore Jamie Grieve sniggering behind his hands with a couple of friends. They'd tease her for days about this.

The bell for the end of school came as a relief and Kate packed her things away quickly, anxious to get out of reach of Jamie and his chums.

David seemed to take forever to get ready, but eventually they were out and walking across the broad, grassy expanse of Bruntsfield Links.

"What happened to you?" David asked, looking at her sidelong.

"I don't know."

"You went really white and just fell down. I thought you'd had a heart attack or something."

"I don't think people have heart attacks when they're our age." She fell silent, deciding whether to tell him about it. "I had a dream or something. Except it didn't feel like a dream. I was in a desert, but it was really cold, and there was a woman ... her clothes were soaking; it was as if she'd just come out of the bath, or out of a river. She knew who I was and I was scared of her, but I wanted to know how she knew me, and then she touched my head, and then I woke up. I suppose all that sounds really stupid?"

David thought. "Not stupid. Just weird. Not your sort of thing." He looked at her hard. "Are you sure you feel all right now?"

"Yes. I was fine as soon as I woke up — apart from feeling like a complete idiot."

They crossed the road and opened the wooden gate to David's garden. As he rummaged through his pockets for the key, Kate said, "Please don't tell Claire or your dad, okay?"

"Okay!" He pushed the door open. "It's just us," he called, dropping his bag and jacket on the floor. Kate followed suit.

There was no answer, but when they got to the kitchen they found a plate of peanut butter sandwiches waiting and through the open door they could see Claire in the back garden, hanging out washing. They started on the sandwiches.

As they ate, Claire came in with the empty laundry basket.

"Hi, David."

He grimaced as she ruffled his hair.

"Hello, Kate."

She put the basket down and watched them eat. "Do they not feed you at school at all these days?"

"Hardly at all," said Kate.

"Just stale bread and water," added David.

"And grey porridge."

"And rotten meat."

"And lumpy custard."

"Bogey soup."

They dissolved into giggles. Claire rolled her eyes.

"You're a right pair of eejits sometimes. What time's your dad due in?"

"About six."

"Better get the tea on then. Are you staying for tea, Kate?"

"Yes, please. My mum's coming over for me about eight."

"Righto."

She moved about the kitchen, humming to herself, as Kate and David finished the last sandwiches.

"How long d'you reckon that homework's going to take?" asked David, round a mouthful.

Kate shrugged. "Half an hour? Bit more maybe. We may as well do it now I suppose."

David heaved a theatrical sigh and carried the empty plate across to the sink. "Thanks, Claire. We'll be in my room."

"Okay, Davie, just call me if you get stuck with anything."

"Ha ha."

"Cheeky brat!" Claire said in mock outrage. Being rude was their way of showing how fond they were of each other. Claire had looked after David for nearly three years now and they knew each other inside out.

Before she'd come, once it was only Dad and him, there had been a succession of women who'd cooked and cleaned and picked him up from school, but none had lasted longer than a year, and most for only a few months. The record shortest stay had been four days, but he couldn't even remember that one; he'd only been five after all.

They retrieved their bags from the hall, went into David's bedroom and re-dumped them on the floor in there. Tiger, David's cat, was curled up asleep among the tangle of clothes and duvet on his bed. He looked up when Kate and David came in and Kate went across to stroke him. "Hello, Tiger. Caught any mice?"

To her surprise, Tiger flattened his ears and drew back from her, hissing. "Tiger? Come on, you know who I am."

But the cat jumped down from the bed and shot out of the room.

"Why'd he do that? Is he all right?"

"Weird. He usually loves it when you stroke him. Maybe you smell funny or something."

"Oh thanks."

"Not that you *do* smell funny; well, not to *me* anyway, but maybe to a cat …"

"David!" She threw a pillow at him and five minutes of cheerful anarchy followed, before they settled down to the awful maths.

"Kate, that's your mum," called David's dad.

"Thanks, Alastair. I'm just coming."

"Lucky for you," said David. "I was just about to bankrupt you."

"No you were not," Kate replied, pulling on her jacket. "Leave the board set up and I'll prove it next time I'm here."

"Are you going to tell your mum and dad what happened to you at school today?"

"Of course not! Don't you dare tell your dad."

"Don't worry."

In the sitting room, Ruth and Alastair were chatting as they waited.

"Thanks for tea," said Kate as she came in. "Bye, David, see you tomorrow."

"Remember about Saturday."

"Oh yes. Mum, we need to go back to the museum. I can go with David on Saturday morning, can't I? There's no football this weekend."

"Can't see why not. This project had better be good, the amount of time that's going into it."

After Kate had gone, David went through to the sitting room again, where his father was emailing friends in Houston.

"Want to say anything to Kevin?"

"Nah."

"I thought you two were friends."

"We were, but what's the point of just emailing each other if we won't see each other any more?"

"That didn't stop you emailing Kate from America."

"That was different. Think how long I've known Kate. Anyway, I knew we were coming back."

"We might not have."

There was a short silence.

"You never told me that."

"I wanted you to see the place and get to know it without automatically hating it. You know you would have, if I'd said we might be moving there for good."

"So why didn't we?" said David gruffly.

"It was never more than a possibility. Things didn't work out."

"Do you mind?"

Alastair swivelled his chair around from the computer to face David properly. "I thought I would, but when it happened, or in fact *didn't* happen, I was relieved. Once we were in Houston, I realized I didn't want to leave Edinburgh. It was fun for a year, but only because I knew we were coming back. I found out about three months into the trip."

He smiled at his son. "Should I have told you all this before?"

David thought for a moment. "I don't know. It would have been nice if you'd talked to me about it, but I'm not sure I would have told me if I'd been you. I'm glad we're still here though." His gaze drifted to a framed photograph on the mantelpiece, the last one of them as a family, taken on some beach on the west coast when he was four and a half. "It's where Mum is."

They both looked at the photo without speaking, then Alastair got up from the computer. "Let's have some supper and I'll thrash you at chess."

4. The Round Room

Saturday morning was bright and chilly — autumn arriving properly at last, said Ruth when David arrived at Kate's house.

It was the noise he always noticed when he was there. There were only four of them, but they seemed to make an incredible din. Even when not all of them were there, it hardly made any difference. Ben made the most noise and Robert, Kate's dad, the least, but people were always talking at once and interrupting. Trying to get a word in was like trying to find a gap in the traffic to dodge across Princes Street.

Kate's dad wasn't there this morning. He ran a decorating business, which — although in theory he didn't do any of the painting and papering himself — seemed to always require his presence to get some job completed by the deadline.

"Come on, we've got to get out of here fast," said Kate.

"Why?"

"Ben's expecting some friends over to play. Trust me, you don't want to be trapped in here with three four-year-olds."

"No way. Let's go."

They walked down through the sloping grassy park called The Meadows, where the inevitable group of people was involved in a rag-tag game of football.

Kate and her dad were avid Hearts fans; not a happy interest the way the league had gone last season. David, who'd never been that keen a supporter, although he liked to play, had developed a taste for

American football during his stay in Houston, which he was maintaining via satellite TV. He was trying to convince Kate of the superiority of the American game and getting nowhere.

"At least come round and watch a match with me and see what you think then."

It was the fourth time they'd had this conversation.

"Okay, I'll watch it, but it won't be a patch on real football," Kate sighed.

They were almost there now, coming up Middle Meadow Walk. They bought sweets at the newsagent to sustain them until lunchtime and were on the steps outside the museum in time to see an attendant unlock the doors at ten o'clock.

One and a half hours later they decided they were finished. Kate gathered up their papers while David put the last touches to a sketch he had done for a picture of a hill fort.

"Good morning, Kate."

Kate looked up, surprised; she hadn't thought there was anyone else near them. She smiled when she saw who it was. "Hello, Mr Flowerdew. How are you?"

"Very well, my dear. And you and the family also I hope? Ah, David, good morning to you. Is that a picture for the project?"

How did he know about it, David thought again, but all he said was, "Yes, just a sketch. I'm going to work on it at home."

"May I see it?"

David opened his sketch pad.

"Ah, yes. A good choice of subject. Plenty of detail to be included if you wish, but it won't suffer if you leave it out. What about the Pictish Stones? You could draw them beautifully."

Kate and David looked blank.

"Don't you know them? The carved stones in the little circular room?"

"I don't think we've ever seen them," said Kate.

"They're just across the hall. Come along, I'll show you."

They followed Mr Flowerdew around display cases through the gallery and into the hallway where the metal men stalked. Mr Flowerdew walked briskly past them to a corridor that sloped gently downwards. Glass cases, set into the white walls at shoulder height, held coins and jewellery — much the same as they had seen elsewhere.

The corridor opened out into a circular room. In a case at the entrance was a crudely carved wooden figure about a metre high, with pebbles for eyes. Beyond it were great carved stones, lumps almost as tall as the children, some covered in spiral or geometric patterns, others with stylized animals: geese, fish or wild boar.

"This is the lowest part of the museum," said Mr Flowerdew as he moved between them. "These are the oldest things. No one now understands what the carvings meant, but they were powerfully made."

As he spoke, Kate was aware of a faint buzzing sound coming indistinctly from all around them, an uncomfortable noise somehow. When Mr Flowerdew stopped speaking, it was the only sound she could hear, although it was so quiet. From the busy museum around them, not so much as a whisper penetrated this room. She looked at David to see if he could hear it too and saw him shake his head as though he was trying to dislodge an insect.

Now the sound was growing stronger. She longed to break through it, but found that she was afraid to speak, afraid to disturb it.

She turned to Mr Flowerdew. He was listening

intently and he looked angry. As she watched, he dropped his walking stick. It fell to the concrete floor with a clatter and Kate and David both jumped forward to pick it up. As they did so, Kate realized the noise had stopped.

David got to the stick first and handed it back.

"Sorry," said Mr Flowerdew. "How stupid of me. Perhaps not the stones after all, eh David? Time we had something to eat, I think. Come along."

And he ushered them somewhat hurriedly past the watching wooden figure and up the short corridor back into the ordinary noises of the museum.

Up in the hallway, Kate said, "What was the buzzing noise back there? You heard it, didn't you David?"

"Yes, it was horrible."

"Mr Flowerdew?"

"Buzzing? Horrible noises?" He looked puzzled. "I heard the air-conditioning, as usual. It certainly disturbs my thinking. Quiet; that's what you need to think properly."

"No," Kate persisted. "Not air-conditioning. Something else."

Mr Flowerdew raised a quizzical eyebrow. "It seems to me that you two have been working too hard and are weak with hunger. I trust your parents would have no objection if I took you both to the café?"

Over cakes and drinks he told them more about the Pictish stones and drew the one with the goose on a page of David's sketch pad.

"Well," he said, laying down the pencil and checking his pocket watch. "I must be off. It's been good to talk to you. I hope to see this great project when you complete it. Perhaps you could bring it round to my house some day? I've got some bits and pieces that you might find interesting."

They agreed and said goodbye, then wandered back to the Main Hall, intent on lunch at McDonald's. As they passed the Information Desk Kate stopped to read something.

"Look at this!" The poster to which she was pointing was advertising a sleepover at the museum in two weeks time. *Arrive with a sleeping bag and a supply of food at eight, get locked in and spend the night.*

"Cool. Can you spend the whole night wandering around?"

They read further. *Torchlight tour of the galleries, breakfast in the Hall and let out between seven and eight the next morning.*

"What do you think?"

"Sounds good to me."

"Me too. Do you think the parents will let us?"

"Can't see why not. We spend enough time here anyway and we'd be locked in. Surely that's safe enough for them?"

"Let's take some leaflets and persuade them."

They were halfway down the steps when they heard barking, quite high-pitched, the sort of noise a small dog would make.

Although they looked around, they couldn't see any dog, large or small, but the barking continued insistently.

"Maybe it's in a parked car," said David, "or it could be lost and hiding under one."

"It sounds so close," said Kate, "but where on earth is it?"

"Here boy," called David, snapping his fingers and crouching to look beneath the cars in the little car park, but there was no dog.

Suddenly the barking stopped and though they

waited for nearly five minutes, it didn't start up again.

"I give up," said David, "Let's go and have lunch."

After one last fruitless look around they set off down Chambers Street. Behind them, at the foot of the museum steps, a small dog sat on the pavement.

5. Fog

The television crew arrived half an hour late. Gordon wasn't that bothered, but the boss seemed to be taking it as a personal insult.

"Do they think we've nothing to do but stand around waiting for them?" Marion Purves fumed, looking at her watch for the tenth time in two minutes. "I've got a stack of letters about a foot high on my desk waiting to be answered.

Right, that's it, I've had enough. Gordon, would you give me a call when — if — they turn up and I'll come down — if I'm free."

"Certainly, Mrs Purves. I'll let you know as soon as they arrive."

Marion Purves turned on the heel of one of the shoes it looked as though she had polished specially for the occasion and headed off down the hall at considerable speed.

Slow down, Gordon wanted to say to her, *and don't get so worked up or your face'll be all red when you do get on television*, but you couldn't really say that to a boss, even one as good-natured as she normally was.

"Gordon!"

Sheila at the Information Desk was pointing to a group of people lugging equipment up the stairs from the front door.

Five minutes later the boss had clicked her way back up the hall to the clock, all smiles now, while the crew unpacked the camera and sound equipment and started checking levels.

"Sorry we're late," said the reporter, a woman called Fiona Mackie who Gordon recognized vaguely from TV.

"The last job over-ran."

"No problem," replied Marion, with an apparently genuine smile. "Wednesdays are fairly quiet."

The camera operator muttered something to Fiona Mackie.

"We're just going to get some general shots first. Let's step away from the clock, shall we? So we don't need the public kept out of the way yet."

They watched the camera operator backing away from the clock, watching the image she was filming.

"We'll do the voice-over back at the studio." She paused, looking at the clock as if she was only now seeing it properly. "It really is something, isn't it?"

Marion nodded in agreement. "It certainly is. The workshop's through in Glasgow, but they used material from all over the place to make it. The wood for the monkey came from the museum, you know; a big lump of oak that was dredged out of Duddingston Loch with some Bronze-Age weapons years ago. It had been sitting in storage ever since. It's nice that they were able to use it.

It took nearly fifteen minutes for them to get their *establishing shots* as they called them, and then Fiona and Marion went up to the first floor to do their bit with the top of the clock in the background. After that they had to block off one of the stairways so Fiona could come down slowly with the clock in shot, explaining more about it.

"Great," she said, back at ground level again. "We'll cut it all together tomorrow or the day after and the piece will go out on next week's programme. Now, what time is it?"

It was twenty-five to four.

"Oh no. We're due in the Signet Library at four, but we really must have footage of the clock striking."

"We can switch it on now," said Marion. "You don't need to show the clock face: it's all the rest that people are interested in. Gordon knows how to trip the mechanism manually, don't you, Gordon?"

"Well, yes, but I'm not supposed ..."

"Oh nonsense, there'll be no problem. On you go, Gordon."

Gordon was not a happy man. Yes, he knew what to do, but you didn't muck about with a mechanism like this unless you had a good reason. They turned off the music at night right enough, but left the working of the figures alone, so that they spun and swung and turned in eerie silence on the hour.

He swung open the side panel and moved all the switches that would bring the clock to life, then stepped back out of shot as the crew filmed the monkey turning her handle.

In the bird biology gallery, a white-haired old man with a walking stick raised his head from a sketch of an albatross, an expression of disbelief on his face.

"Fools," he muttered to himself. "What are they doing?"

When they'd all gone and Marion had retreated to her office, Gordon reset everything and hung around with some anxiety until he had seen the clock behave as normal when four struck, before he went for his tea break.

The old man watched it carefully too, shaking his head gently once or twice. He waited until every bell had stopped trembling, then walked slowly away and out the front door, leaning more heavily than usual on his stick.

At the bottom of the steps he paused, listening to the sound of a small dog barking. The dog itself was nowhere to be seen.

"You know too, don't you? You heard it and knew it

was the wrong time. Where have you gone, I wonder?" he said, half to himself, as he walked away.

Gordon's shift finished at six that day, once all the doors had been locked and all the galleries and toilets and cloakrooms had been checked to make sure there wasn't some fool hiding, intent on spending the night as a bet. It was surprising, or maybe it wasn't really, how often that happened.

He went for a couple of pints in Sandy Bell's with some of the lads when he'd finished, so that it was nearly eight o'clock when he came out into the misty evening and decided to walk down the hills home to Stockbridge.

In summer, the place would have been busy with tourists, but now at the start of October, in the quiet between the Edinburgh Festival and Christmas, there were only a few people walking along George IV Bridge. He reached the traffic lights and looked left up the hill towards the rearing bulk of the castle, then right towards St Giles with its stone crown illuminated against the sky, less distinct than usual because of the mist, which seemed to be getting thicker.

Across the road he went past Deacon Brodie's pub then down the steep hill called the Mound, with its views away over Fife. Not that you could see that far tonight of course, in this mist.

As he walked down the hill he saw that it had gathered thickly in Princes Street Gardens, lying in their hollow beneath the castle rock. He could see it moving in rags and tatters down there, something shining beneath it.

Shining?

He stopped and looked again. There it was, like a gleam of light reflected from water, only there was no water down there, hadn't been since they drained the Nor Loch, nearly two hundred years ago. Now there were the railway lines and the gardens, but no water, except in a big fountain at the far end.

Even knowing that, it still looked wet. The mist had drawn back in places and he could swear he was looking at a rippling body of water. There were sounds too, like the splash of oars and muffled laughter.

This couldn't be happening. He was having a dream and he'd wake in his own quiet bed, far away from impossible water.

But he knew he wasn't dreaming.

He'd only had two pints. He couldn't be drunk and hallucinating. Sober and hallucinating then?

There was another sound from below him as though oars were being shipped and a boat being bumped ashore out of the shallows and at that moment Gordon was rocked by a cold wave of fear. It brought him to himself. He began to walk fast, crushing the desire to run, the hair rising on the back of his neck.

He went fifty yards, almost to the junction with Princes Street, where other people were walking, off out for the evening, then stopped and forced himself to look again.

Princes Street Gardens lay calm and dim under a sky clear of mist; battalions of roses, tall trees and wide lawns all as they should be. He stared and stared until he became aware of a passing couple looking curiously at him and roused himself to continue walking.

There was no explanation for what he'd just seen and heard except some sort of hallucination. What was happening to him? Maybe he was coming down with the flu. That could be it.

He'd go home and lock the doors and windows carefully and fight it off with a big whisky.

6. *The Sleepover*

"Mum! Ben won't get out of my room. He's messing up all my stuff," Kate yelled round the door of her bedroom, holding on to a squalling Ben by a handful of sweatshirt. "Ouch! Mum, he's kicking me."

Ruth emerged from the study just as Ben dissolved into theatrical sobs and Kate let go. "Come on, Ben. I thought you wanted to make biscuits. Leave Kate alone, she's trying to pack."

The sobbing stopped abruptly. "Is she going away? Can I have her room?"

"I'm only going away for one night, idiot. I already told you about it."

"Don't call him an idiot," said Ruth mildly. "It's only half true. Come on, Ben."

Kate shut the bedroom door. Why was it always so hard to get any peace or privacy in this house? Sometimes it felt as though she lived with about twenty people, not just three.

She found herself envying David and his dad and then felt awful that she'd done so. She knew how lonely both of them had been since his mum died. Neither of them said so any more, but she could see it in their eyes sometimes when they were round here and didn't know she was paying attention: a longing as they watched Mum and Ben.

She checked her bag once more, then went to see if there were any bits of biscuit dough that needed eating.

"Here they are," she called from the window where she'd been keeping watch for the last ten minutes.

"A kiss, a kiss," yelled Ben, suddenly agitated in

case Kate disappeared without saying goodbye.

Mum and Dad, to her relief, didn't make a fuss over her going, just a quick kiss each and a reminder to thank Alastair for taking them.

At the museum, they found a parking space just across from the main entrance and joined the trickle of people carrying sleeping bags and backpacks.

"I have to come and sign you in and leave emergency numbers," said Alastair, "but don't worry, I'll push off as fast as possible. I don't want to spoil your fun."

Inside the Main Hall it was darker than they had expected, only a few lights shining, the brightly lit Information Desk like a beacon, and as they went in the last few notes of the clock's performance were dying away as it settled into quiet for the night.

Once Alastair had filled in a form signing them over officially, he gave David a quick hug and strode off to the door without looking back.

"Dump your stuff over there with the rest just now and have a seat," said the tall, dark-haired man at the desk. "There's another three to come and then we can get started," he added.

Kate read his name tag: G. Syme. "Can we sleep *anywhere*?" she asked.

He laughed. "No. We don't let you near the mummies, if that's what you're about to ask. We don't want you scaring each other to death during the night. You can sleep here in the Main Hall, or in with the elephants or the British mammals or the fish. Fish or mammals are comfiest because there's carpet on the floors."

"All right, Sandy?" he asked a smaller, balding man who'd joined him at the desk as he was speaking.

"Aye, Gordon. Fine."

"I'm away to sort the clock for the night. There's

still three to come," said G for Gordon and set off up the hall with a big torch in one hand.

Kate and David sat down on one of the padded benches by the fish pool, eyeing the others already waiting there.

"Twenty-one," said David.

"What?"

"People. And three to come makes twenty-four. Should be plenty of room, even if everyone decides to sleep in the same place."

Three girls appeared up the steps from the front door, carrying rucksacks that made it look as though they'd come to stay for a week, accompanied by someone's anxious-looking mum. She went through the form-filling, then an elaborately affectionate goodbye that left one of the girls scarlet with embarrassment.

"Okay," said Gordon. "Good evening everyone and welcome to the museum sleepover. Anyone been on one before?"

A couple of boys raised their arms.

"You can just doze through the talk then, lads. It'll be the same as you heard last time."

He went on to explain where they could sleep, what they could and couldn't do and so on. "Right. You've got ten minutes to go and reserve your spot for the night then back here for the VIP tour. Bring your torches."

There was a scrum as everyone rushed for their belongings and groups separated off to each of the sleeping areas. Kate and David had decided on the British mammal hall and they made a little campsite by the seals, friendly faces, David thought, if they woke in the middle of the night.

Apart from them another two pairs were settling themselves in the room, one beside the dolphins, the other by the white cattle.

Back at the desk, Gordon and Sandy were counting heads. When a trio of boys appeared from the direction of the fish gallery, Sandy gave Gordon a nod and led them through a pair of tall wooden doors that said "Staff Only" and into the working heart of the museum, where animals went for taxidermy, fabric for conservation and pottery to be dated; a brief glimpse of each so that no one got bored. Round a corner they came to a table covered with cans of juice, pizza and chocolate biscuits, and for ten minutes they sat on the floor or leaned against the wall, happily pigging out.

"Well," said Gordon, "are you ready for the spooky bit?" There was a chorus of affirmation. "Torches on then. This is when the lights go out."

As he said it, the lights did go out and there were a few squeaks of mock alarm.

"Nobody gets scared too easy, do they?" asked Sandy.

"Nah."

"Not likely."

"Course not."

"Switch on your torches then," he continued. "Everyone ready?"

They filed out into the new, dark museum, Gordon leading and Sandy making sure no one got left behind, whether by accident or on purpose.

It was a moment before Kate realized they were in the Main Hall again. The yellow beams of light from the torches didn't penetrate very far, but there was a half moon sailing high above the glass roof, giving just enough light to show faint outlines of the fish pools and the clock.

Gordon led them up the steps to the first floor and into the costume gallery, where blank-faced figures watched them from the display cases. It *was* quite spooky, Kate had to admit, especially when she noticed one figure in a yellow dress and hat, craning forward as though for a better look at them. No one talked above a whisper now, apart from a few slightly nervous laughs.

From there, they went to what everyone assumed would be the creepiest bit: the Egyptian section with its bound mummies and painted sarcophagi. For Kate it was a bit of a disappointment. If you were on your own in the dark it would be really scary, but with twenty-five other people so close it didn't seem much different from how it was during the day, just darker.

Someone's torch picked out a mummy with gold feet and a gold mask where his face would have been. He had huge ears and a daft smile that made him look like a cartoon character. Kate pointed him out to David and they were overcome with a fit of the giggles.

Last, they went to the dinosaurs. The skeletons looked bigger than they did in daylight, especially the Ichthyosaur, hanging above them as though still swimming.

"You can have a wander round here for five minutes. Down or up one level's all right but *don't* go out of this section on your own."

People spread out slowly. Kate and David joined the group that headed upstairs. There were big skeletons up here too: giant sloth, armadillo and elk, magnified by torchlight, but there were much smaller things also: beautiful Eskimo carvings of bone and walrus ivory. Kate's favourite was an otter lying on its back and she moved away from the others to look at it now. It looked so funny, with its hind legs curled up and its front paws at the sides of its head as though it had just heard bad news.

As she looked at it, she had a sudden sensation that someone was standing just behind her. She turned, expecting to see David, but her eye was caught by the reflection, in a display case, of something moving, low and fast. She swung round with a gasp.

"David, did you see …?"

Her voice died away. There was no one there. She could make out David, with some of the others, at the other side of the gallery. She swung the torch from side to side, the hair rising on the back of her neck.

She forced herself to walk slowly over to the group, heart thumping in her chest as she tried to calm herself and pretended to listen to their discussion. It was no good: the feeling that someone else was there wouldn't go away.

"Kate?"

She jumped slightly when David spoke.

"Are you okay?"

"Can we go back down now? Its cold up here," she lied as she shivered.

She was going to tell David about the feeling, but it went as soon as she started down the stairs, so suddenly that it stopped her in her tracks for a couple of seconds.

Fool. Scaring yourself over nothing.

She could almost believe it was true.

7. Biscuits

It was eleven thirty when they finally began to settle themselves in their little bivouacs. A few lights were on around the place so that if anyone woke disorientated during the night — assuming anyone slept — they wouldn't be panicked to find, for instance, an elephant gazing down at them out of the darkness.

Kate and David lay caterpillared in their sleeping bags, eating and talking. Despite the unexpected earlier supper, they had plenty of room left.

"Did Claire make this?" asked Kate, round a mouthful of chocolate cake.

David nodded and after a few seconds, swallowed. "I made the icing though." He licked a blob off one thumb.

"It's really good." Kate dug into her bag again. "Ben made us biscuits," she said, rolling her eyes. "I had to bring them or he'd have had a fit."

They looked into the plastic box.

"They're interesting shapes," said David slowly. "What sort of biscuits are they?"

"He said they were Action Man biscuits. Mum helped him with them so they're probably not actually poisonous."

David chose a small one, looked at it a bit more closely, then took a bite.

"Well?"

"Quite good actually. Orange. And there are bits of nut in them. At least I hope they're bits of nut. Bit crumbly," he added, as the rest of the biscuit disintegrated all over him. "Yuck. It's gone inside my sleeping bag. I'll have to get out and empty the crumbs." He took another biscuit and put it all in his mouth at once. "Safest way to eat it."

Kate put the box of biscuits down beside her backpack and watched as David flailed around with his sleeping bag trying to get the crumbs out.

Things had gone quiet around them now, as people began to think they might actually try to go to sleep. Kate checked her watch — ten past midnight.

"I'm going to sleep," she told David as he crawled back into his de-crumbed sleeping bag.

"Me too," he replied. "Don't want to be falling asleep at football practice tomorrow."

She smirked. The likelihood of anyone falling asleep within range of Mr Davidson's voice was nil. He could have coached them without leaving his house at all, he was so loud. He would definitely pick on anyone who yawned their way through a practice though.

David was squiggling around beside her, trying to get his pillow the way he liked it. Finally he was satisfied and they lay staring up at where the ceiling would be if you could see it. It was very quiet now; whatever was going on in the other sleepover areas, everyone in this one had settled down for the night. Kate snuggled further down into her sleeping bag. It was surprisingly comfy. She could almost imagine she might eventually fall asleep.

She stood in a wasteland of blowing sand, shivering and alone. She had been here before; she recognized the empty white view stretching away forever all around her.

This time, no figure appeared in the distance moving towards her. She simply turned and the woman was there in front of her, two or three metres away. Behind her stood a pair of dogs.

She looked as she had the first time Kate had seen her, water trickling from her hair, hands and clothes, her dress stuck wetly to her legs, her too-vivid mouth smiling.

"Go away," said Kate without thinking. "Get out of my dream."

The smile stretched wider.

"Who are you? At least tell me that."

The woman shrugged. "I have had many names. Why does it matter if you will not talk to me?" Behind her the dogs watched intently.

Kate forced herself to turn round and walk away, concentrating on trying to wake up.

The woman was in front of her again, blocking her path. "Talk to me. We are alike, you and I. I could show you such things ..."

"Tell me your name."

"If it matters so much to you, you may call me Tethys. We have been waiting for you for so long, Kate."

"We?"

"My ... family ... friends. Waiting for you to help us. And now the time is coming. Now the time is close when we shall walk together and everything will change. Everything. You cannot imagine, Kate, what it will be like. Let me show you."

She held out one dripping hand. Behind Kate, one of the dogs began to howl, and she realized they were not dogs, but wolves.

"No!"

Kate must have shouted out; shouted so loud that she woke herself, struggling to sit up in her sleeping bag. She fumbled for her torch and switched it on.

Beside her David slept, a frown on his face. If she

moved the torch beam round she could make out the humped shapes of the others across the room.

She was safe in the museum. Safe. She thought about waking David, but before she had the chance the light from a more powerful torch than her own swung around the room and there was Gordon.

"Everything all right? I thought I heard someone shout."

"I think it was me. I had a bad dream."

"You're not the first. This place can do that."

"No. It's a dream I've had before. I don't think it's anything to do with being here. I'm fine now I've managed to wake up."

"Sure?"

"Yes."

"Anyway, I'm just out there if you want me." He gestured to the hall.

"Thanks. I'm fine. Goodnight." She turned out her torch, lay down again and watched the light disappear with Gordon before she closed her eyes.

David knew where he was at once.

He was looking down. Between and around his booted feet were small, smooth pebbles, grey and white and black. He knew that if he raised his head he would see the lake stretching away in front of him, still and shining like an enormous coin, but he didn't want to see it. There was something *wrong* about the lake.

He began to walk along the pebbly shore, still looking down at his feet, looking down because that was safe, because he was afraid of what else he might see if he looked up, who might be there beside him, watching the silver lake.

The sensation that someone else was walking there with him was becoming stronger, but he could only hear his own feet on the pebbles, even when he slowed or paused.

The person who wasn't there was between him and the lake. David stopped and screwed his courage tight and turned slowly until he faced it directly.

No one.

Nothing but the endless sheet of glittering water, with violet mist at the edge where it faded from sight.

Now that he was looking at it, it was difficult to stop. He stared, imagining how it would feel against his skin if he simply walked in. Not cold, he was sure of that, though he had no idea why. Perhaps he would float on it like a leaf.

At the very edge of his hearing was a sound somewhere between buzzing and whispering, a disquieting sound, growing very slowly louder. It came from his left and he found himself straining to hear, yet not wanting to at the same time. He was sure it came from who, or what, had walked beside him earlier, and was now standing a little way off to his left.

He refused to turn his head. With a desperate terrified conviction he was sure that as long as he didn't see what was there it could not be real. If he didn't turn his head he was safe.

He had no idea how long he stayed like that, trying not to hear the whispers. He was very tired.

Eyes fixed on the pebbles, tracing the veins in one after another, he tried to shut out that other presence, until a tiny movement caught his eye and before he could stop himself his head turned reflexively to follow it … and he found himself looking at the toe of a hiking boot.

"David? … David!"

"Mmmn …?"

"You were mumbling. You woke me up," hissed Kate.

David came fully awake, looking round for a moment in confusion. "Sorry," he said. "I was dreaming."

"I know. I heard you."

"What time is it?"

"Just after five. Go back to sleep."

He tried.

At six o'clock they both gave up and started rummaging for left-over food.

"We didn't finish Ben's biscuits, did we?"

It took a moment for the increasingly feeble torch beams to find the box. It was empty.

"Did you eat them during the night?" asked Kate, accusingly.

"Of course not. I wouldn't have finished them. Maybe you ate them in your sleep."

Kate snorted. "Well, somebody ate them."

They sat in a moody silence, on the verge of an argument. Across the room, the others were still asleep.

Later, when the lights were on and they were packing up, David suddenly said, "Kate, look."

There was a trail of Ben's crumbly biscuits running from where the box had been, up onto the display platform and across the pebbles to a gap between two of the seals' rocks.

They looked at each other.

"Do you think it was a rat?"

"I don't know."

They crept forward and bent down slowly, craning to see into the crevice, but there was nothing there.

Alastair was waiting at the front desk, as arranged, to sign them out and swap their football gear for their overnight things. They told Mr Syme about the biscuit trail, but he looked at them as if they were having him on, although he did promise to go and take a look.

"Have a good time then?" asked Alastair as they went out.

"Yeah, it was great," said David. "Lots of extra food too."

"Do you *ever* think about anything else?"

"Sometimes."

"Enjoy the football. See you later." Off he went to the car, laden with rucksacks and sleeping bags.

As it was early, there wasn't much traffic around, so they heard the sound of barking as they went down the steps, even though it sounded as if it was further away this time.

"Do you think it's the same dog?"

"Dunno. Sounds the same. Where is it?"

They stood in silence, trying to locate the source of the sound.

"Over there," said Kate, pointing. "It's across the road in the churchyard."

They crossed the road and followed the sound of the invisible dog. Once inside the churchyard they stopped again, listening.

"That way. Look, there he is."

A little dog lay on the short turf in front of a gravestone. He quietened when he saw the children approaching, thumping his tail on the ground instead, but he wouldn't come to them.

As they walked towards him, Kate said, "Listen."

"What? There's nothing to listen to."

"I know. That's what I mean. It's awfully quiet; there's no traffic noise at all."

They reached the place where the dog lay, and

played with him and stroked him for a few minutes, but he wouldn't leave the grave.

"Let's go, shall we?" asked David. "It's *too* quiet. It's a bit creepy somehow."

"Yes. Come on."

They walked quickly back towards the gate, staying close together. As they reached it, the unnatural silence stopped quite suddenly, as though someone had flicked a switch, and the normal sounds of the city were restored.

They looked at each other.

"What was that all about?"

"I don't know." Kate was looking at the statue, which stood just across the road from the churchyard entrance — of a little dog; a rough-coated terrier of some sort.

"You don't suppose ...?"

David followed Kate's gaze.

"No ... no, that's ..."

"Impossible?"

"Yeah."

Once the last of the children had been picked up, Gordon and Sandy went to check the places they'd slept and pick up the inevitable litter. Two of the kids who'd been in the mammal hall had made up some story about a rat. Gordon could see a scatter of crumbs and pieces of biscuit. They'd made it quite convincing, leading under the artificial rocks where a real animal might take food.

He crouched down, and shone his torch in for a good look. There were some more bits of biscuit in a corner by the mountain hare. The cleaners wouldn't be pleased. He straightened up and saw as he did so a little paw-print on the glass at the front of the display. Not a rat; it was too big for that. A little hand-print rather that a paw-print.

He remembered half-seeing something whisk out of sight behind a display case that night a couple of weeks ago, and shivered without knowing why.

8. Mr Flowerdew

Mr Flowerdew lived in one of a terrace of houses with small gardens in front and long ones behind. Ruth insisted on coming to the door with them. Just to say hello, she said, but Kate thought she wanted to make sure that he remembered inviting them.

The iron gate squeaked on its hinges as David pushed it open and they walked up the path under a rowan tree weighted with ripening berries. The door opened before they got to it.

"Good afternoon," said Mr Flowerdew. "A squeaky gate is sometimes an advantage. I am often able to surprise guests, even when they mean to surprise me. Come in, come in."

He ushered them into a hall dominated by a grandfather clock with a deep, slow tick, its face enamelled with stars and moons.

"That clock," he said, seeing them study it, "is exactly as old as I am. It was made for my birth and set going on the day I was born — a family tradition. It has never stopped since."

"My goodness," said Ruth, "how impressive. I don't remember seeing it before."

"It isn't always here."

What an odd thing to say, thought David. It would be very difficult to move.

"Anyway," Ruth was saying, "I must be getting along. It's very kind of you to invite them. I'll be back about seven."

"Splendid. Goodbye for now."

He saw her out, then turned back to the children. "Come into the drawing room first."

It was a big room with a bay window, and from the fireplace a wood-burning stove threw heat to every corner. Tall bookshelves took up one whole wall, and another was almost completely covered with paintings and sketches and photographs. There was a music system with shelves of CDs beside it and, more surprisingly, a wide-screen TV.

"I enjoy watching films," Mr Flowerdew said when he saw them looking at it, "and many of them don't look their best crushed onto a square screen."

David had moved across to the wall of pictures. "Look — it's us!"

And so it was. The two of them, aged five, shining clean in new uniforms, ready for their first day at school.

"I remember Dad taking that photo," said Kate.

"Me too. He got really annoyed because we wouldn't stand still."

"Weren't we small? Yet I remember thinking I was so grown up because I was starting school." Kate's gaze drifted upwards. "There's Grandma."

Grandma Alice beamed out at them, as blue-eyed as her granddaughter, seated on a straight-backed chair with a very new baby in her arms.

"Who's the baby?"

"It's you, Kate."

Mr Flowerdew was looking at the photo now.

"Is it? I've never seen this photo before."

"No. I took it, and this is the only copy. You were just a week old when it was taken."

Kate studied her tiny self with interest, not that she could see much: just a squidged-up face and one fist. Grandma looked very happy, holding her with practised ease. Round her neck Kate could make out the gold necklace that was now her own.

"Now where have I put my reading glasses ...?" He patted his pockets and looked around the room. "Hmmn. They must be upstairs. Bring the project up and we'll look at it in my study."

The study was up two flights of stairs, and they settled there like birds amongst a fabulous clutter of objects.

An astronomical telescope stood ready by the window, with binoculars and a small notebook nearby on the windowsill. From the mantelpiece, a stuffed tawny owl surveyed the room. Its breast feathers, when Kate touched it, were impossibly soft. There were more shelves of books — many about natural history — and a neat stack of sketchbooks with a little set of watercolours beside them.

Beside the tawny owl were a number of small objects: little carvings, mostly in wood, but a couple that looked like ivory.

"Look, Kate," said David, who had come over for a closer look. "Isn't that the same as the one you like in the museum?"

He was pointing at a tiny otter, back legs curved, front paws pressed to the side of its head.

"Oh yes! Is it all right to touch it?"

"Go ahead. It's survived hundreds of years of quite rough treatment. I doubt you could hurt it even if you tried."

Kate carried it to the window where the light was better.

"This is my favourite thing in the whole museum. Oh — there's a hole through it."

You couldn't see the hole unless you turned it over to see the bottom, which would have been the otter's back.

"It would have been a fastening for a coat originally:

like a toggle. There would have been a piece of sinew or something of the sort through there to attach it."

"I love the way it holds its head in its paws."

They wandered about the room, looking and touching to their hearts' content as Mr Flowerdew read the project. When he finished, he said, "It's excellent; just as I thought it would be. Strange, isn't it, to think that we live in the same places they did, that are so different now. What would we each do if we came face to face, I wonder?" He took his glasses off, and chewed reflectively on one of the legs. "Did you know there was once a big settlement on Arthur's Seat?"

David nodded. "Dad told me a bit about that." He hesitated for a few seconds, then plunged on, "When we met you at the museum — not when you took us to see the stones — the first time. You knew about the project but we hadn't told you. How did you know?" His heart was beating fast.

Mr Flowerdew beamed. "I am very old. At my age you know a great many things without having to be told. It is one of the few advantages of the ageing process."

It wasn't an answer, but it was all that he got before Mr Flowerdew changed the subject.

"It's time I started to make tea. Come down to the kitchen; I'm sure I bought some food and drink for you."

In the big kitchen he rolled up his sleeves, tied on a long white apron like French waiters wore in films, and Kate and David busied themselves with coke and chocolate biscuits while he made an enormous pizza.

He saw them share a look of surprise as he worked. "What? You think old men can't make pizza? Just you wait!"

Once it had gone into the oven he poured himself a

big glass of red wine. "Did you know it's good for the heart?"

"Dad always says that too," said Kate.

They ate the pizza blistering hot. There was more than they could manage. When he was utterly, totally full, David said, "Thanks. That was delicious."

Kate mumbled agreement through her final mouthful.

Mr Flowerdew was silent, twirling the stem of his glass between his fingers so that the wine spread in ruby veils up the sides. In the quiet, the ticking of the grandfather clock sounded very loud, and when Kate looked at Mr Flowerdew's face he seemed suddenly sad and far away.

As though he sensed her watching, he looked up, straight into her eyes, unsmiling, something more than the old friend of her grandma's she had always known.

He sighed. "And now, Kate, David, there are some things I must tell you."

They looked at each other and then back at Mr Flowerdew. What could he mean? For a moment there was silence except for the tick of the great clock.

"Time," began Mr Flowerdew, "goes in one direction only, does it not? From the past to the future, no turning round, no going back."

"Well, yes, of course," said Kate.

He shook his head. "It is not inevitable that it should behave like that, and there are some whose greatest desire is to see it change. If they were to have their way, time would come unstuck; past and present would be jumbled together."

"But that's impossible," said David.

Mr Flowerdew shook his head again. "Not impossible, only unimaginable, but if the Lords of Chaos ever have their way, that is what will happen. Opposed to them are the Guardians of Time, who fight to keep the stream of time flowing smoothly. This is a conflict that has gone on since the world first formed and will always continue, unless the Lords of Chaos win and time spins out of control forever."

The children exchanged glances and Kate shifted uncomfortably in her seat.

"Oh come on, that's not true. You're just making it up as a joke. Why are you saying all this? Anyway, how would you know about it, or why wouldn't everybody know about it?"

"I know," he said gently, "because *I* am one of the Guardians of Time.

"You ask why everyone would not know about this war — for that is what it is. The answer is that people are blind to most of what is around and in front of them. Sometimes a battle breaks through into the human world, and appears as a war or plague, or some event which no one can explain, but your race forgets the true significance of things quickly.

"You think I'm a delusional old man, who's raving," he said with a smile, "but *think*. Remember what happened in the room with the Pictish stones."

Kate's eyes widened as she remembered the strange buzzing. How could she have forgotten that?

"The dream," said David wonderingly. "It's something to do with the dream I've been having, isn't it?"

"Tell me," said Mr Flowerdew.

He described the lake and its stony shore and, his voice a little unsteady, his fear of the unknown presence. "I'm scared I'm going to see whatever it is before I can wake up."

Mr Flowerdew steepled his fingers and sat in silence for a few seconds. "What about your dream, Kate?"

"How did you know?" She hadn't meant to sound angry, but she did.

"From your face. Tell me, please."

So she described the desert and the wolves and the dripping figure of Tethys.

When she had finished, he drew himself up straight in his chair. "This is one of the occasions when the war between Chaos and Time is breaking through to your world. I'm not surprised you both dreamed in the museum, for it is the focus of what is happening."

"Why?" asked David, drawn along, for the moment, with the old man's story.

"Power! It is a focus because of all the powerful objects held there. This power has been building up for years, like water behind a dam, and since the Duddingston Hoard was found ..."

"The Duddingston Hoard? What's that?"

"To the eye, nothing more than a cache of old and broken weapons; but the power of the Guardians was poured into some of those weapons at their forging, for they were made for one of the great battles between Time and Chaos, three thousand years ago. After the battle, they were thrown into the loch to take them out of the world of men and dissipate their power. They should not have been taken from the loch. Now there is too much power for the dam to contain and it has begun to leak; in Edinburgh, time is coming unstuck.

"It has always been a city where the past has left a strong imprint, and it is easier here than it would be in most places for the Lords to open the door to the past a little. We push it shut from the present of course, but it is slowly opening, and the past is rising up all around us."

He rubbed a hand across his face, as though he was suddenly very tired. "I'm truly sorry that I have to involve you in this, but there is no help for it. I know that what I say sounds incredible, but please think about what I have told you and consider whether it could be true, because without your help, I do not know how the Guardians can force the door to the past shut."

"Our help?" It was Kate who spoke. "How could we possibly help? We're eleven years old."

"I don't want ..." Whatever Mr Flowerdew was about to say was interrupted by the ringing of the doorbell. He looked at his watch in surprise. "It's later than I thought," he said. "That must be your mother, Kate. All I ask is that you think about what I have said and, if you decide it could be true, let me tell you more about it. Now, Kate, you had better let your mother in."

Kate got up slowly, dazed with words, and went to the front door. David made to follow, but Mr Flowerdew put a hand on his arm. "David, I know your dream is frightening you. It cannot hurt you, I promise you that; but as long as you are afraid, it has power over you. Next time it comes, raise your head and find out who is there with you."

"You two are very quiet," said Ruth on the way home. "Is something wrong?"

"No."

"Nothing's wrong."

"What did you do?"

"We looked round the house — there are loads of interesting things."

"And he made really good pizza for tea."

"And we talked."

"Yes, we talked."

"That's all."

9. Discussions

Mary Sinclair locked the door behind her and put the key in her pocket. It was a beautiful bright autumn morning, a touch of frost in the air. She could see her own breath and that of the dog hanging in the air as they walked into Holyrood Park and up the path towards Dunsapie Loch.

Once they had crossed over the road she took off Holly's lead and the Jack Russell ran off up the hill at once, barking happily. Mary stayed just above the road, breathing the sharp air deeply, knowing that Holly wouldn't stray too far.

The dog began to bark again, as though she'd seen a rabbit — common enough up here. Mary looked to see where she was; while Holly was normally obedient, she might well take off after a rabbit.

The dog was standing still, hackles up, barking furiously at something on the skyline, not a rabbit after all. Mary squinted up; she really should get glasses, she couldn't see very clearly at that distance.

"Holly, stop barking! It's just people out for a walk, like us."

Five people were silhouetted against the sky. She couldn't make sense of their clothes, they looked odd somehow; and they were carrying long sticks.

"Holly!"

The dog wouldn't stop barking; Mary climbed up to where she was and clipped the lead back onto her collar, then looked up again.

They were still there with their sticks, sharp against the skyline in a huddled group. The low sun glanced off the end of one shaft as though there were metal there.

Mary felt the hair rise on the back of her neck.

"Come on, Holly," she said quietly, pulling on the lead. "Let's go home now."

As the pair of them headed back down the hill she glanced over her shoulder frequently, watching the figures on the horizon until the slope of the ground hid them from view.

"Well, what do you think?" David tore off a piece of bread and threw it into the water for the ducks to fight over.

It was the day after their extraordinary visit to Mr Flowerdew. When Kate had phoned David to suggest a walk to Blackford Pond he had accepted at once.

There was an eruption of quacking as three mallard laid claim to the same piece of bread.

Kate shook her head. "I don't know what to think. He's probably just a crazy old man, but ..."

"But everything fits, doesn't it?"

"It's still impossible. It must just be a whole lot of coincidences and him trying to entertain us with a story or something. He's probably having a good laugh at us right now."

David looked at her, but she wouldn't meet his eyes. Instead she reached into the bag for another piece of bread to give to the geese milling about their feet.

"You don't believe what you're saying," David said.

She threw down the handful of bread she'd been holding. "It can't be true. This sort of thing only happens in TV programmes."

"Okay. What about the dreams we've been having?"

"Coincidence."

"And what happened in the room with the stones?"

"Oh, I don't know." Kate pushed her hair behind her ears and reached for another slice of bread.

"I'm scared too, you know," said David. "The dream scares me. I don't want to go to sleep, even though I haven't had it again since the museum."

They moved away from the geese and began to walk slowly round the pond.

"Just say it *is* true," mused Kate, "then why us? There's nothing special about either of us, and Mr Flowerdew must know that."

David didn't reply.

"We have to go back and see him again, don't we?" she went on. "We have to find out more: hear what he has to say and then make up our own minds. I bet if we go back there ready for what he might tell us we'll realize he's just a silly old fool."

Still, David said nothing.

"You believe him already, don't you?"

"Sort of. I don't know why; it's just a feeling. Maybe you're right: it's all a story and the dreams are just dreams. I hope you are."

They had reached the far end of the pond.

"Do you want to go up the hill?"

"Okay."

There were rough steps up the side of the hill, their cut earth stabilized by old wooden railway sleepers. When they got to the top they turned to look over the roofs and trees spread below them. It was windy up here, though it had been calm enough down by the pond. There were a few brambles still clinging to their thorny stems, missed somehow by those who descended with bags and bowls as soon as they were ripe. Kate pulled a few to eat, but they were half dried out and had lost their sweetness, and she threw them down the hill instead.

"Okay. We need to see Mr Flowerdew to sort all this out," said Kate. "Can we just tell our parents we want to go and see him again? They might think that's odd — after all, we've known him for years without wanting to go and see him all the time."

"Yes, but we'd never been to his house before and it *was* really interesting even if nothing had happened, and your mum knows him really well; it's not as if he's some stranger we want to see."

"I suppose so." Kate shivered. "It's getting cold. Let's go back."

By the time they reached David's house they'd come up with a way of asking to visit Mr Flowerdew without seeming desperate, but their inventiveness was wasted. The first thing David's dad said when he opened the door was, "Mr Flowerdew's just been on the phone. You forgot to take that set of oil pastels away with you, David. I said you'd go round on Wednesday after school to get them. He seemed to think you'd be going as well Kate, but you'd better check that it's okay with your parents. You didn't say anything about the pastels when you got home, David."

"Ummm … no, I forgot."

"It's not very good manners to forget when someone's given you a present. Make sure you apologize on Wednesday."

"Yes, I will, Dad."

Safe in David's room they exchanged wide-eyed glances.

"There wasn't any set of pastels, was there?"

"No. I would hardly forget to take something like that with me."

David flopped onto his bed, kicking off his shoes.

Kate sat down next to him. "You'd almost think he knew we were trying to find an excuse to see him."

"He did."

"What?" She turned to look at him properly.

"Well, can you think of a better explanation?"

"It could be a coincidence. Maybe he meant to give them to you and forgot."

"Yeah, right. Come on, Kate, you don't believe that any more than I do. Why won't you be honest with yourself about this?"

She turned away to the window and looked out over the garden, struggling with herself. Finally, she said:

"Because if I keep pretending, then maybe none of it will be true. I wish I'd never heard what he told us yesterday. I want life to stay normal."

"So do I," David said from the bed, "but if what he told us is true, then pretending isn't going to help, is it?"

10. The Monkey

She had waited so long to be out in the light; to hear, to taste air; such a long time.

They had taken the wood and carved her and she had waited patiently to be freed by their tools, as she had done already, century after century, and at last there she was: complete and carved, coloured and gilded, with gold on her wrist as she deserved.

She had thought she was free, and they had thought she was their prisoner, and they were both right and both wrong. When she had discovered what they planned, when they trapped her in place, she would have howled if she could, but they had not carved her a voice.

At first she tried to be content out in the light, hearing, tasting air, but she wanted to be free. Truly free.

They had not realized, of course, how she would focus all the power from round about on herself. Stupid. So she waited again, still patient, feeling the power loosen the trap around her, until the first night her spirit stepped free, and left the carved image standing there.

There were many places in the museum where a small monkey could hide unnoticed.

11. *The Task*

The squeaky gate did its work again and the door opened as they walked under the rowan tree. Mr Flowerdew gave them a brief smile as they entered the house.

"Thank you for coming back," he said, and handed a small package to David. "The oil pastels you're supposed to have come to collect, in case we forget later."

"Thanks." David put them carefully away in his bag.

"Come up to the study."

Accompanied by the deep tick of the clock, they went upstairs. Mr Flowerdew waved them to a couple of armchairs but remained standing himself, looking out of the window down the long garden.

After a minute he passed a hand over his face and turned back to the room, pulling an old wooden swivel chair away from the desk for himself. "Is there anything you want to ask?"

They looked at each other.

"No. We want to hear what you have to say first, then we'll ask."

"Very well." He drew a breath. "I am one of the Guardians of Time. There are several hundred of us around the world, always watching for signs that the Lords of Chaos are trying to break through into this existence. The war between the Lords and the Guardians has gone on since time began to flow here, and now we are both bound to this planet.

"We have feared for a long time that they would attack again in Edinburgh. The past and present are only loosely anchored here — partly because it has been a battleground for us before — so two or three

Guardians have made it their home, until now. Now we are stretched so thin that I am the only one.

"I have lived here continuously since 1348 by your reckoning. I have been John Flowerdew for eighty-two years now — the longest I have been any one person. I was born as him so that I could come to know your grandmother, Kate. We thought for a long time that Alice would turn out to be the one, but we had the generations wrong: you and David are the keys, not her."

"What do you mean, we're the keys?" Kate asked incredulously.

"From time to time certain people are born whose fate it is to aid or thwart the attempts of Chaos to destroy time. You and David are two such people. Look ..."

As he spoke, the room turned misty around them, and in the mist they saw figures, people dressed in skins, standing on the edge of a loch. Behind them, a great fire burned down to embers.

A woman and two children moved away from the group towards the pyre and bent to pick up ash and smear it on their faces. The children were crying, the tears making streaks through the ash. Their faces were so alike it was obvious they were brother and sister; the girl about eight and the boy six or so.

The three of them walked back to the water's edge where a man and another woman waited and bent to pick up objects from the ground. One by one they threw them into the water, light glinting on the metal as they did so; axe-head, spearhead, knife-blade and lastly, the broken remnants of a sword, were all cast away by the children.

The mist swirled more thickly and the vision faded, and they were once more in Mr Flowerdew's study.

"How did you do that?" asked David, wide-eyed.

"That does not matter. It is what you saw that is

important. That was the aftermath of the first great battle of the Guardians and the Lords in Edinburgh — at Duddingston Loch. The weapons you saw thrown into the loch are part of the Duddingston Hoard."

"But what does it have to do with us?" Kate asked, baffled.

Mr Flowerdew held up his hand. "You are the descendants of the children you just saw: the *last* descendants in Scotland apart from Ben. They were the children of the man who made the weapons, the village Smith — and he died during the battle.

"But we're just friends. We're not related."

"You are, but very distantly. You share the Smith's children as your ancestors. The Hoard must return to the loch, and the two of you must do it; that is why you are the keys."

There was a moment's silence, as they tried to digest what they had just seen and heard.

"You said earlier aid *or* thwart. You mean we could do either?"

"Yes. You could be the means whereby the Lords triumph, or by which we defeat them once more. Make no mistake; both sides will seek to persuade you to help them."

"What if we decide not to be on anyone's side?" asked David.

Mr Flowerdew looked uncomfortable. "I wish I could say you would be left alone to get on with your lives, but I am afraid you are too valuable to both sides for that to happen. You are unavoidably a part of this. You cannot watch from the sidelines." He gripped the arms of his chair hard and got to his feet. "I am sorry. I thought there would be more time before we had to call on you, but the Lords have stretched us so thinly that we can barely contain them. If there had been another one of us in Edinburgh we might have been able to hold them off without your help even yet … The echoes of the past have grown so strong since the Millennium. There were never so many minds focused on time before … and the clock in the museum draws power to it like a magnet, and has become a tool to help the Lords open the door to the past. When its time was disordered for that television programme it helped their cause even more.

"We are already fighting as hard as we can to close the door to the past. We need your help, or it is likely that we shall be defeated."

Breaking the tense silence that followed, Kate spoke.

"What happens if you win?"

"Nothing. That is, no one would be aware of it, because time will continue to flow unchanged."

"And if you lose?"

"Then the world that you know will cease to be."

There was silence, for what seemed like a very long time, before, finally, Kate spoke again. "How do we know what to believe? It's all so … Is there any proof?"

"None at all. The only real proof will be in your heart, if you recognize the truth. I would guess though that your dreams have not returned since we last spoke."

They shook their heads.

"Why does that matter?" asked Kate.

"If the dreams continue to develop you would be more likely to believe me, but that is not what the Lords want. If they are just bad dreams and they stop, then perhaps I'm just a silly old fool."

Kate coloured, although he was carefully not looking at her.

"You are more likely to be taken in by them if you have dismissed me."

"Are they here, like you?"

"No. They are *confined* in a different dimension. They cannot reach you physically, but they can influence you. They will try to pressure you to help them, by threat or promise."

"But isn't that what you're doing?"

He sighed. "It must seem so, but we aim to protect the world you know; the Lords mean to destroy it. Which would you rather see happen?"

There was a trace of impatience in his voice for a moment, but when he spoke again it was gone.

"I'm sorry. It is unfair of me to expect you to decide quickly — or at all. Come down to the kitchen and I'll find you something to eat, and then you can talk to each other in peace while I tidy the garden."

In the kitchen he made a pot of tea and produced a sticky lemon sponge, dripping with icing. He pulled on a pair of wellingtons and a very grubby jacket and unbolted the back door. "I'll be about fifteen minutes," he said as he went out.

At first, they concentrated on their slices of cake, avoiding talk, but the final crumbs were soon gone.

"It's true, you know," said David. "I can feel it. I can't explain it, but I'm sure. And how did he show us that ... whatever it was ... if he's not what he says he is?"

Kate pushed her hair behind her ears. "I know. I've been trying to convince myself that I don't feel like that, but I do. I only wish I didn't believe him. 1348 did he say?" She shook her head as though trying to clear it. "I can't work out how old that makes him."

"So we help?"

"If we've decided he's telling the truth, how can we not help? But what can we do? There's nothing special about us."

"He seems to think there is."

Kate cut an extra piece of cake for each of them and they ate in silence.

They jumped when there was a knock at the back door. Mr Flowerdew put his head around it. "Can I come in? Or would you like more time by yourselves?"

"No, come in. We took more cake — I hope you don't mind."

"Goodness, no."

He wrestled his boots off, then his jacket, washed his hands, poured a cup of tea and sat down, looking from David to Kate and back.

David nodded that Kate should speak for them both.

"We believe you. We want to help, but we don't see how we can."

A smile of pure relief lit his face. "Thank you both. You don't yet know how much this means. Thank you." He took a drink of tea, collecting his thoughts. "Our problem is that the museum is brim full of power, which is focused by the clock into a form that the Lords of Chaos can use. We must disconnect this power so they can no longer reach it. There are two things we must do to accomplish that: the Duddingston Hoard must return to the loch and the clock must be changed — its spirit must be constrained."

"Spirit? You mean like a ghost?"

"No indeed. More like a soul. You have seen the monkey at the bottom of the clock?"

They nodded, intrigued.

"She is carved in the form of an ancient Egyptian spirit, but more important than her form is what she is actually carved *from*. Look again."

Mist obscured their surroundings once more and they were back on the loch edge, watching the children hurl the pieces of the broken sword into the water.

This time though, they saw what happened next: two young men wrestled a great tree stump into the loch.

Abruptly they were back in the study.

"The monkey was carved from the oak stump on which those weapons were forged. Some of their power flowed into it. The anvil should also have stayed hidden from the world, but it was dredged up with the weapons and shaped into the monkey. She is the spirit of the clock, and the power that was in the weapons has shaped itself into consciousness in her. Now she calls their power to herself and her strength grows. She is close to escaping the clock altogether, and if she does so, all the pent-up power in the museum will tip into Chaos. Already she moves away from it sometimes in the night, creeping through the museum. Soon she will grow bolder.

"We must bind her to the clock for good, while we have the chance."

"How do we do that?" asked Kate.

"You already have the means, although you do not know it. Kate, you have a necklace of your grandmother's, do you not?"

"Yes," she said, her brow creasing. "How did you know?"

He smiled, the first time he had really looked untroubled all that day.

"I know, because I had it made and gave it to her, and asked her to leave it to her first granddaughter. It was made fifty-four years ago for this moment, to bind the monkey to her place in the clock for all time."

"But the clock wasn't made until 1999."

"But I knew it would be."

Kate shook her head, completely baffled. "So all I have to do is put the necklace on the monkey and that's it, everything's fixed?"

He gave a short laugh. “I wish it was so simple. It must be done in the right way at the right moment by both of you working together. Only together will you be strong enough.”

“Wouldn’t it be better to get some of the other Guardians to come to help instead of us? Then you’d be sure of winning, wouldn’t you?”

“If Edinburgh were the only battleground that might work, but each one of us faces a part of this struggle wherever we are. The truth of it is that there is no one who can leave their own fight to lend us help here. The four of us must accomplish this alone.”

“Three of us, you mean.”

“Four. Only three as yet, but we need a fourth. We must find someone inside the museum who will work with us and help us steal the Duddingston Hoard so we can return it to the loch.

If we can do both these things, the past should sink to its rightful level again and this particular threat will be over.”

“So now you have to try and persuade someone at the museum about all this?” said David. “How are you going to do that? It was hard enough convincing *us*.”

“It may not be as difficult as you think. Already there are rumours about a small animal which leaves its traces in the museum but is never clearly seen, and a feeling of disquiet is growing among those who are sensitive to what is happening.

“I’ve been a regular visitor for a long time. The staff are used to talking to me.”

Mr Flowerdew looked at the children’s bleak faces and said gently, “We have some time before we will be forced to act.”

“Oh good,” said Kate weakly. “Enough time for us to grow up?”

"A few weeks."

"Oh. Right."

They sat in silence round the big wooden table until David said, "We should be going."

"Of course."

Numbly, they gathered their belongings.

"I'll be in touch soon, but if you want to talk to me before that, just telephone."

He opened the front door.

"And by the way, I think you know me well enough to call me John, don't you?"

"John?"

"Even a Guardian of Time needs a first name. You don't imagine everyone calls me Mr Flowerdew all the time?"

"John."

12. Latin

Princes Street Gardens hadn't played any nasty tricks on Gordon Syme after that singular occasion, and yet he found himself increasingly unsettled.

The few times he'd walked down that way after dark the weather had been clear, and it had been obvious that the valley below the castle held only railway tracks, grass and trees. Yet he found himself on edge, listening for the muffled splash of oars and gruff voices, and felt shameful relief if he found himself walking past the gardens with others.

So it was that on Tuesday night, when he left to walk home after a drink with the others — just like the last time, he thought — he was pleased when he realized that the person who'd fallen into step beside him as he walked along George IV Bridge was someone he recognized, and who also recognized him.

"Mr Syme, isn't it?" said the man. It was the old gent with the sketchbook who often sat in the Main Hall.

"That's right — Gordon. I recognize you from the museum, don't I?"

"Yes. John Flowerdew." He held out his hand to shake Gordon's own. "I should have introduced myself long before now. Would you mind if I walked with you? I think we're both going the same way."

"Not at all. The company's welcome."

"It's a fine night for walking."

"Beautiful. I often think the town looks its best on a clear night."

"I believe you're right. Night covers the ugly details rather well for the most part, and the skyline gets to speak for itself."

They walked on in silence until they had crossed the road at Deacon Brodie's pub, which was raucous already, although it wasn't yet nine o'clock.

As they started down the hill, the old man said, "Strange isn't it, how the mist gathers in the valley like that? You'd hardly believe the main railway line was down there."

Gordon felt his heart give a thud as he looked towards the gardens. The mist rolled across them in coiling white clouds.

"It must have been quite a sight in the old days," John Flowerdew went on, "before they drained the Nor Loch. I believe they held frost fairs on it in the fifteenth century when it used to freeze solid. Now that is something I would like to have seen."

As he spoke they continued to walk steadily down the hill beside the misty gardens. Gordon's mouth was dry. *Don't be ridiculous*, he told himself. *It's just mist. There are still the gardens under it. Don't be stupid. Just look.*

He forced himself to turn his head to the left and concentrate sight and hearing on what might lie beneath the mist.

A train whistle made him jump, and at that moment a veil of mist blew aside and he saw not water, but the familiar outlines of trees and grass.

He realized he'd been holding his breath and let it out, cursing himself inwardly for being so stupid. How had he come to be so afraid of something that wasn't even there?

John Flowerdew didn't seem to have noticed anything amiss with his behaviour and was talking on serenely about frost fairs.

They crossed Princes Street and walked up to the top of the next hill.

"Our ways part here, I think. I've enjoyed the company. Thank you," said the old man.

"I'm sure I'll see you at the museum soon," Gordon replied.

"Oh yes, very soon indeed." Mr Flowerdew cleared his throat. "There are very few people to whom I would say this, but you are, perhaps, someone who would understand."

Gordon waited to see what was coming.

"Sometimes at night, in the mist, when I go past the Gardens, I am sure the Nor Loch has returned. I see it and hear it. I hear men in boats on it — I even smell it. I don't know how to explain it, but it happens."

Gordon felt as though someone had flung icy water into his face.

"Anyway, I mustn't keep you any longer with a foolish old man's fancies, Mr Syme. Goodnight to you."

Gordon mumbled some sort of goodnight and stood rooted, watching the old man make his steady way along George Street.

What was happening to him? Was he going mad? How did the old man know what he'd seen and heard? He found that he was shivering, although the evening was not cold.

Automatically he turned his footsteps towards the home that no longer felt safe to him.

The next few days did nothing to settle his mind. The cleaners were gossiping openly now about there being some wee animal loose in the museum that no one could catch, an animal that scattered crumbs and opened drawers and left handprints on glass. He'd seen the prints and crumbs himself, of course, but since that night no one had got any sort of glimpse of an animal.

It wasn't just him that was spooked by whatever it was. Some of his colleagues were even less willing than usual to do their turn at night shift, but would not admit why. Only Sandy remained unmoved by the idea of the "wee rat," as he called it, roaming the museum happily in the darkness.

"D'you reckon we'd get any sort of reward if we caught it?" he asked Gordon one afternoon.

"Don't be daft. There's nothing to catch."

Sandy opened his mouth to retort, but Gordon had escaped by going to help a man emerging from the Staff Only door, almost hidden by a large polystyrene box.

"Need a hand with that, Mr Nixon?"

A face peered round the box, light brown hair flopping down to round spectacles.

"Oh, Gordon, it's you. Yes please. It's not heavy, just awkward. I think your arms are longer than mine."

"What is it today, Mr Nixon?"

"Birds. Waders mostly. We had a lot handed in after the storm last month. I've not had a chance to take a proper look at them yet. Thought I'd just take them home and do it there."

"Are you in the front car park?"

"What? Oh yes, thanks, but there's no need..."

"No trouble, Mr Nixon."

By the time Gordon returned, Sandy had forgotten what they'd been talking about, and the rest of the day passed quickly, and on the way home there was no mist.

At least, there was no mist in Princes Street Gardens ...

Down by the shore at Cramond, the lights of the houses and the pub failed to penetrate far through the haar that had drifted in off the sea and wrapped itself coldly round the village.

The top of the tower house poked out above the mist like a stumpy finger, its windows showing clear as a lighthouse.

Inside, Andrew Nixon was finishing his preliminary examination of the batch of frozen birds he'd brought home. There was nothing outstanding, but they could do with some new specimens of Turnstone and Redshank, and he'd do the others as skins for the reference collection.

He left the two he wanted to work on the next day in the specimen fridge to thaw slowly and put the others back in the freezer. He'd long ago got used to the bad jokes people made when they heard that he worked as a taxidermist: quips about putting sage and onion stuffing in instead of straw, or eating the bird he was working on for the museum, instead of the one he'd roasted for Sunday lunch, and he no longer noticed how odd his house must look to visitors. Living there alone, as he had done for years, he had it all arranged to his own taste, which probably wasn't shared by that many people.

Furniture, carpets, curtains and the like didn't much interest him; so long as they did what they were meant to he saw no reason to change them, and the house had a shabby look to it as a consequence.

However, he did care about his books, and they were carefully housed in the floor to ceiling shelves he'd had built specially.

His true passion, of course, was the stuffed animals, and their glassy gaze dominated every room. Some were Victorian, rescued from junk shops or bought at auctions; then there was the collection his father had amassed in much the same way. Lastly, there were his own specimens. Birds mostly; they were his favourites — the delicacy and balance of them posing a perpetual challenge of positioning them so they looked truly lifelike. He always thought of himself as being in pursuit of the perfect specimen, never quite satisfied with what he produced.

Under the critical gaze of a crow and two field voles, he heated some tinned soup and made toast. He'd meant to shop on the way home, then realized he didn't dare keep the specimens in the car for that long. This sort of thing was happening too often. Maybe he should get a housekeeper, then he could come home to a lit fire and the prospect of a proper meal.

He went through to the sitting room to check on the progress of the coal fire he'd lit half an hour before. It was drawing well now, the coals glowing red, and he decided to bring his frugal supper through here. He went across to the window, set in its eighteen-inch-thick wall, to draw the curtains.

Below him, mist lapped the tower like water, opaque and milky. On impulse he pushed the window up, listening for the sound of the sea a hundred metres away. It was a calm night, and the unseen water made small shushing noises against the rocks as the tide fell. It was overlaid by other, closer sounds, which Nixon strained to hear.

The area between the tower and the shore held some scrub, a small car park, and one corner of the building site where they were installing the new sewage treatment plant. Normally it would be quiet at this time of night, but it sounded as though a large number of people were gathered down there in the mist. He could hear shouts and laughter, and the sound of metal striking metal. Now that he looked more closely at the mist, he thought he could see the flicker of flames through it.

Normally, he would have closed the window, drawn

the curtains and forgotten about it, or if it was something which worried him he would have phoned the police, but now he found that almost without thinking about it he had pulled the window closed and gone down the twisting stairs to where his coat was hanging.

He was out of the door before it occurred to him that these people, whoever they were, might not be pleased to see him, and that really, what he was doing was most unwise. However, his feet kept carrying him towards the noise somewhere on the building site.

There was definitely a fire — no, fires — flickering through the mist in several places. It dawned on him that he shouldn't be able to see them. There should be a four-metre plywood barrier around the site.

They must have torn it down. They were probably vandals, or travellers maybe. He'd better watch his step. He continued to move forward cautiously. He could hear the voices clearly now, but couldn't make out what they were saying; in fact it didn't sound like English at all.

He could see figures, gathered round the fires indistinct through the fog. There seemed to be tents too, and he could smell meat cooking. He caught another snatch of conversation, strange and yet familiar in its pattern of sounds. The figures he could see round the fires seemed to be wrapped in blankets, as if this were some sort of camp for the homeless people he normally saw bundled up in doorways in the city centre.

Moving carefully, he stepped over the boundary where four metres of plywood should have stood.

At once, the mist was gone, and he stood frozen to the spot, looking around him. Now he knew why the language had sounded familiar and what it was.

Latin.

He stared about him at a Roman army camp —

tents, cooking fires, soldiers in rough woollen cloaks playing knucklebones. Had he wandered onto a film set? If so, where were the lights and cameras, and why were people speaking Latin? He felt his hackles rise at the profound *wrongness* of the scene.

Just then, a soldier at the nearest campfire looked up and straight at him. Nixon saw his eyes widen with fear as he jumped to his feet, knocking the knucklebones flying. Following his gaze, his companions were standing up, making the sign against evil with the hands that weren't reaching for weapons.

Andrew Nixon ran. He ran as he had never run in his life, blood pounding in his ears, back to the thick-walled safety of the tower house, fumbling with his keys and pushing the door shut with his full body weight, turning all the locks and bolts, to stand trembling in his dark hall, listening in terror for the sound of Latin beyond the door.

There was no noise of pursuit. After two or three minutes he climbed the stairs on shaking legs under the impassive yellow gaze of his birds. In the sitting room the fire still burned, and its crackling was the only sound he could hear. He went to the window and peeped around the edge of the curtain, then pulled it open, his senses reeling.

Under a clear night sky, a four-metre barrier of plywood marked the boundary of the building site with its cranes and heaps of earth. There was no sign of the Roman camp.

13. *Lightning*

"I'm whacked," said David to Alastair, yawning ostentatiously. "I'm off to bed."

Alastair opened his eyes wide in a pantomime of disbelief. "Are you all right? It's not like you to volunteer to go to bed — especially recently."

"I know. No, I'm fine. I just need a bit of extra sleep. You should be pleased; it's what you're always telling me to do."

"Don't get me wrong. I *am* pleased. Goodnight then."

David gave his dad a rather furtive kiss. "Night."

In his bedroom he found Tiger sprawled on the bed. He lifted the cat off and pushed him out of the room, closing the door to make sure he stayed out.

When he looked out of his window he saw a clear, cold night, the street lamp shining at the end of the garden. He pulled the curtains closed, undressed and got into bed.

In spite of what Mr Flowerdew had said, he was scared. He could feel his heart thumping faster than usual when he thought about what might happen once he fell asleep.

Remember, he thought, *it's just a dream. Nothing can hurt you.*

He closed his eyes.

The mercurial expanse of the lake stretched flat before him, the far shore indistinct. Pebbles moved under his feet as he turned slowly three hundred and sixty degrees, straining his eyes and ears.

He was alone. Away from the lake's edge, the pebble

beach stretched back into the distance, the stones becoming larger the further from the water they were, until there was a landscape of boulders.

There was no sound, no movement. He was definitely alone.

He began to walk along the shore, feeling the rounded shapes of the pebbles through the soles of his shoes. He let his path veer closer and closer to the water until he was barely a hand span from it. It was unnaturally still, not the tiniest ripple disturbing its eerie perfection. As he looked at it, the buzzing started, and he felt the hair rise on the back of his neck.

He kept walking slowly, not letting his pace quicken, and this time instead of trying to block the sound out, he strained to hear the whispering voice.

"Come to us. Be one with us. We can heal your pain. Listen. We understand. Come to us."

"Don't be afraid. Don't be afraid," he muttered to himself under his breath. He stopped walking and listened carefully to gauge the direction from which the voice came.

To his left. Definitely to his left. He let himself take three deep breaths and turned very slowly to face the source of the sound … and thought his heart would stop.

A figure stood on the lake, perhaps five metres from the edge. Not in it, but *on* its surface, not disturbing the flat calm in the slightest.

It was a man, tall, with greying black hair and a beard, dressed in a ragged black robe, which fluttered in the wind.

There *was* no wind, David realized, but the robe moved anyway, and the man's hair blew back from his face. His eyes, David noticed, were a very bright blue.

He stood quite still, in the wind that was not there.

Silver rivulets from the lake began to slowly climb the tatters of his robe, like the shoots of a plant. Only his mouth moved in time with the whispering, buzzing voice, but the movements of his lips didn't quite match the words; like a piece of film with the sound and vision out of synch.

All that David wanted to do was turn and run with his hands over his ears, away from the figure and the silver tendrils writhing impossibly up from the flat lake. But he forced himself to stand still, listen and look.

The figure on the lake raised one arm and beckoned to him.

"Come to me. Do not fear me."

David shook his head and despite himself, took a step back, pebbles skittering under his feet.

The crawling silver trails had reached the man's shoulders, and now they turned and began to move down his arms. As they did so, the air around him began to crackle slightly, adding to the weird buzzing of his voice.

For the first time in the dream, David found his own voice. "Who are you?" he shouted, and it sounded flat and small in the dangerous air.

The figure smiled. "I have many names and no name. Who am I indeed?"

Still there was the odd dislocation between the sound of the words and the shapes his lips made.

David watched in scared fascination as the trickles of shining liquid reached his wrists and ran down his hands to hang from his fingertips.

Somewhere far off, thunder growled, and the man with blue eyes began to walk across the surface of the lake, the wind that wasn't there ruffling his robe.

"I can't do this. I'm too frightened," David muttered

desperately to himself as the distance between them melted away.

The man reached the shore and stepped onto the pebbles. Thunder cracked, much nearer now, and lightning flew up from his hands to the sky.

Not water, David thought: *a lake of lightning. Help me please, someone.*

The man stopped on the edge of the shore. "Don't be frightened. We mean you no harm. Come to us. Be one with us." And all the time the gleaming tendrils of lightning crawled across his robe and leapt crackling from his fingers.

"I'm not frightened," said David, in a voice that didn't even convince himself.

Unexpectedly the man smiled, showing white teeth. It was the sort of smile a wolf might have given. In a fluid movement he sat down cross-legged on the pebbles and was still, but for the lightning dripping from his hands.

"The man who calls himself a Guardian of Time has spoken of us, has he not?"

"John Flowerdew? Yes."

"John Flowerdew." He ran the words around his mouth as though he was tasting them. "So that is what he calls himself. Doubtless he has told you terrible things of us, told you that we want to use you to destroy your world, to destroy time."

"Yes."

"And doubtless you believed him. He is very plausible. They all are in pursuit of their own ends; but did he tell you how he plans to use you?"

"Yes. And he told me that you can't harm me. You're just an illusion."

The man raised an eyebrow. "Then at least he has told you something that is true. Of course I cannot harm you. This is a dream. But even if you and I were really here, I would not seek to hurt you. I need your help. Why then would I harm you?"

As he spoke, his voice lost the buzzing undertone and his words and his lips finally matched.

David shrugged. "I don't know. What do you want? Why are you in my dream?"

The man's eyes widened in seeming surprise. "You ask me why? It is you who have called me here."

"I did not," protested David, taken aback.

"Ah, but you did." The man settled himself more comfortably on the shore, shedding small bolts of wild-fire as he did so. "I could not be here otherwise. Your dreams all come from within you. Did your Guardian of Time —" he shaped the words as though they were distasteful "— not tell you that when you asked him about this dream?"

David shook his head slowly.

"You did not call on me by any name, but your longing called me as a magnet calls to iron."

"What longing?"

He narrowed his eyes, looking intently at David, then raised a quizzical brow again. "You truly do not know? I had not thought it possible when there was such strength in your call. Who else is in this dream with us?"

"No one." He remembered. "I mean I don't know — I haven't seen them."

"Has the Guardian put such fear into you that you will not look up in your own dreams?"

"No! He told me not to be afraid, that I should face you."

"He was right. You see, nothing has happened to you. But did he not tell you to face your other dream people too?"

"I suppose he meant me to."

"Perhaps not. He may have realized what it would mean for you."

"What do you mean?" By now, David had almost forgotten to be frightened.

The man shrugged. "I do not know. Remember, this is your dream."

From behind David came a noise of slow footsteps on the pebbles, coming closer. The lightning man was looking past him. "Well David, will you look?"

Don't be afraid. Nothing can hurt you.

His gaze on the ground, David turned and slowly raised his head.

A hiking boot.

He kept his eyes on it for a dozen heartbeats, fearful and eager, then lifted his head further.

Jeans.

A red fleece.

A woman with brown hair brushing her shoulders.

She smiled. "Hello David."

It was his mother.

He stared and stared until his eyes pricked with tears. It was his mother just as she was in the photograph on his own mantelpiece, as she had been before she had died, when he was only five.

He couldn't speak.

He'd tried, so often, to dream about her, but he never could. He talked to her in his head at night, before he went to sleep, going over the times he remembered with her, trying to make it happen, but it never did, not once.

Until now.

"Who is this, David?" asked the lightning man.

He didn't take his eyes from her face, but he found that he could talk again. "It's my mum."

Still his mother smiled at him, not moving. He began to walk towards her slowly, fearful now that she would disappear, that he would wake up. As the distance between them grew less, his steps quickened, until he flung himself into her arms and they collapsed in a heap onto the pebbles.

Tears poured down his face as he held her tightly, and she stroked his hair and hugged him close, calming him as though he were five all over again.

Minutes went by, perhaps hours; he had no idea of the passage of time as he sat with her arms around him, hearing her voice again at last.

Behind her voice there grew a ringing, buzzing sound, different from the one he had heard earlier. It got louder, making it more and more difficult to hear his mother's voice. For as long as possible he ignored it, but at last it drowned her out completely, and he opened his eyes to look for the source.

He opened his eyes: and was in his bedroom, alone, the alarm clock ringing.

"No!"

14. The Old Ones

Gordon was feeling happier than he had for weeks. He wasn't jumpy any more, and had no sense that he ought to be looking over his shoulder, or worrying that he might glimpse something inexplicable from the tail of his eye.

Two gloriously uneventful weeks had passed since his unsettling conversation with John Flowerdew. There had been no mist, no sounds of oars. The mysterious rat, or cat, or … cat that no one ever quite saw seemed to have gone, and the cleaners had stopped whispering about strange handprints on the display cases.

Life was back to normal.

There had been a sudden late influx of tourists this year, and all the staff had been kept busy for the last week answering questions about the exhibits and reuniting families who'd become separated among the maze of stairways in the new part of the building. There was a new exhibition going up too, in the hall between the main gallery and the café, and although it wasn't officially part of his job at all, Gordon always seemed to get roped in to hold something, or shift a case or check that a photo was straight. Not that he minded. A bit of variety was always welcome.

He checked his watch. Break time, thank goodness. He was gasping for a cup of tea.

As he pushed open the heavy Staff Only door he heard someone behind him and turned to find Andrew Nixon, briefcase under one arm, hair awry as usual.

"Afternoon, Mr Nixon. Haven't seen you around recently."

"Hello, Gordon. No. Took a bit of a holiday. Went to stay with my sister in Devon. I decided I'd been working too hard. I thought ..." He paused.

"Yes?"

"Ummm ... no, never mind." Nixon smiled and shook his head. For a moment he looked as though he was about to say something else, but he must have changed his mind, and they went through the door in silence.

In the staff room, Sandy, who should have been back on the public floor five minutes earlier, was sitting engrossed in the football report in *The Daily Record*.

Gordon kicked his foot as he went past. "Come on, Sandy. I know it's a rare treat to read about a match that Hibs have actually won, but you've still got a job out there you know."

Sandy didn't take his eyes off the page he was reading. "At least Hibs win sometimes. Remind me: where are Hearts in the league?"

Gordon put his hand to his heart as though he'd taken a mortal blow. "Oh, you're a cruel man, Sandy" — he grabbed the paper from Sandy's hands — "but our public could be away with half the exhibits while you sit here gloating. Get away with you."

Sandy got to his feet grinning and went back to work.

Gordon started to read the match report on Hearts *versus* Aberdeen as he drank his scalding tea, but he gave up in disgust after a couple of paragraphs. Sometimes the score was all you needed to know.

In a corner of the room Andrew Nixon sat cradling a mug, staring out of the window at nothing in particular. He was thinking about going home, back to the tower house by the Cramond shore. He'd not set foot in it since the morning after he'd had the hallucination of the Roman camp, when, following a wracked and sleepless night, he had thrown some clothes in a case and set off for Devon, too scared to wait for darkness and mist again in that place.

He told himself he wasn't worried any more, that he knew it was nothing more than a waking dream, the result of over work. Everything would be fine tonight. Indeed, sitting here in familiar day-lit surroundings, the whole thing seemed completely ridiculous, and he couldn't imagine why he'd been so frightened.

What he ought to do of course was go there now, with hours of light left, and walk right round the site so that he knew exactly what everything should look like in darkness.

That was what he would do. He'd just collect his mail, then go straight home, and everything would be fine.

The old man stood face to face with the lion, which held a screaming figure clamped in its jaws. Neither of them moved: the lion because it was carved from stone, the old man because he was waiting. It did not trouble him to wait. He could have stood unmoving for minutes or years; it was all much the same to him. He wanted to talk to Gordon Syme and to talk to him in this part of the museum, where the power was greatest and the stirrings strongest.

So he waited, moving around only as much as was necessary to avoid drawing attention to himself. That meant hardly at all, for it was easy to make people's notice slide over you as though you were hardly there.

There he was.

Gordon came slowly down the steps and began a professional dawdle through the tombstones down to the end of the gallery.

As he neared the lion, he realized that the figure next to it was John Flowerdew, apparently engrossed in studying some detail of the carving. He experienced a strong urge to turn and disappear round a corner before Flowerdew spotted him, but even as the thought occurred, the old man looked over and smiled.

Gordon's face formed itself into an appropriate expression. "Mr Flowerdew. Good to see you. How are you?"

"Very well thank you, Gordon. Do please call me John. It's a remarkable thing, isn't it," he continued, "that something as large as this could lie undiscovered somewhere as busy as Cramond for all that time."

Gordon regarded the lion. "Makes you wonder what else is lying around undiscovered, certainly."

"It does, doesn't it? A lot of the things here," — he waved his hand around to indicate the whole floor of the museum — "must have just looked like muddy rocks when they were found. I'm sure people find it hard to believe that they've found something out of the ordinary, or that something extraordinary could happen to them."

Gordon had to try hard to take that as a chance remark.

"I came down here to look at the Duddingston Hoard, but I can't quite remember where it is, I'm afraid."

"Well, that's certainly something I can help you with. It's just down here." Gordon led Mr Flowerdew to the short corridor that sloped down to the circular chamber, warded by its wooden figure. "Just round here."

They stood together at the display case, which held the hoard of broken weapons.

"I wonder what they were like, the people who made

these?" mused Gordon. "I often think about all the people who made the things we have, the glass and the steam engines and the swords and the furniture."

"Probably they were very much like us, if you discount the differences that clothes and language make. People don't change very much at heart."

"I suppose not."

They stood in silent contemplation of the drowned hoard from the loch. After a few seconds, Gordon looked up sharply, frowning.

"Is something wrong?"

"No," he said uncertainly, looking up at the ceiling. "Do you hear that?"

"Hear what?" asked Mr Flowerdew, glancing about.

Gordon began to walk round the chamber, still looking up. "There must be something wrong with the air-conditioning." He shook his head as though trying to clear it. "What an awful noise. That's never the air-conditioning."

Mr Flowerdew stood quite still in the centre of the room as Gordon moved around the edge, pale and looking more distressed by the second.

"Can you hear that? Can you hear them, the voices? What's happening?" He was backed up against the curved wall now, eyes wide, sweating.

Mr Flowerdew looked up at the ceiling and closed his eyes.

The noise stopped.

Gordon licked his lips and swallowed, breathing hard. "What on earth was that?"

"There are things you need to know, but not here." He glanced round. "We should leave this place now."

Gordon walked on shaky legs back into the main corridor, faintly surprised to find that everything looked normal.

"You finish in what … two hours?" Gordon nodded dumbly. "I know that strange things have been happening to you. I can explain what is going on. Will you meet me in the Elephant House Café when you finish work?"

"All right," Gordon sighed.

At twenty past six, Gordon pushed open the door of the Elephant House. He'd spent most of the previous two hours trying to decide whether to come or not, and he wasn't sure he'd made the right choice. He had no idea what had happened in the round room, but he couldn't deny that something had. Put that together with the other recent goings on and you had a puzzle that needed to be solved.

He walked through the busy café to the quieter area at the rear, with its big wooden tables. John Flowerdew sat alone at one of them, doing *The Scotsman* crossword. He looked up as Gordon approached, folded the paper away and rose, smiling. 'Gordon, thank you for coming. Sit down. What will you have?"

"A coffee please." He took his jacket off, suddenly conscious of the museum uniform beneath it, and sat looking round at the other customers while he waited.

Mr Flowerdew returned after a surprisingly short time with two mugs of coffee and a plate of shortbread. "They let me jump the queue," he said. "I come in here a lot."

Gordon stirred sugar into his coffee and accepted a piece of shortbread. "You know things have been happening. You said you could explain them."

Gordon focused on the old man properly, suddenly seeing him quite differently. The nape of his neck prickled, and he found he had sat up straighter, as though under inspection. The man before him was old, certainly, but no fool, and not one to suffer them either.

"You've worked in the museum for some time. You know it well, know what it contains. There are many powerful objects from different times and places. Now there is too much power, and it has begun to seep out. The clock is part of it: it is acting like a lens, focusing this drifting power on the past, allowing it to leak into the present. That is what has been happening. When we were looking at the Duddingston Hoard earlier you heard something that frightened you. You heard the spirits of the Old Ones — the people who made the things in that room. You heard the echoes of a great battle that took place three thousand years ago. You have seen the Nor Loch come back. You know that something moves through the museum at night; not a cat, nor a rat — they don't leave handprints. It is the spirit of time loose in your building: the monkey from the clock.

"This is only the start of what will happen. It must be stopped or time will fly apart like a shattered plate."

Gordon burst out laughing, causing people at neighbouring tables to glance up from their own conversations. John Flowerdew did not join in. He gazed at Gordon calmly enough, but in his eyes was a flicker of anger. Gordon's own laughter spluttered to a halt, and he stared back, angry at himself for getting mixed up with this tomfoolery.

"Whatever's happening, it isn't that. Maybe I'm having some sort of breakdown, and that's why I've seen and heard these things. As for what goes on the museum — it's an old place; I'm prepared — just about — to believe in ghosts, but a wooden monkey coming to life and scampering around leaving hand prints? Come off it." He pushed his coffee away and stood to put on his jacket. "I don't know what made me think you could explain anything. It was a mistake coming here. Goodbye."

As he turned to go, John Flowerdew said, "You came because you already know, deep down. You can only deny the truth for so long."

In Cramond Tower, Andrew Nixon stood in front of his sitting room window staring at the red velvet curtain, as though trying to see through it. It was seven o'clock, already dark outside. He'd been standing here for almost ten minutes now, listening intently for anything that sounded like Latin or the clink of metal on metal, but there had been no sounds other than the normal ones of cars and the sea and a couple of dogs barking as their owners took them for their evening walk.

All he had to do was look out of the window and see everything normal, and the stupid thing would be over.

His hand shook as he took hold of the heavy red velvet. He eased it open a fraction and peered out, unaware that he was holding his breath, and then pulled it all the way back.

Under a clear sky he could make out the empty car park that lay below the tower, and to the right, the jumbled shapes of the building site, patchily illuminated by security lights, and perfectly, blissfully normal.

Anger powered Gordon all the way to Princes Street, past the fog-free Gardens — no sign at all of the Nor Loch. It wasn't until he had to stop and wait to cross the road there that he began to calm down.

The old man must be touched, that was it, no point in being angry with him. Still, how had he known about what Gordon had seen and heard in the Gardens? And what had gone on in that room this afternoon?

It was all rubbish, that's what. Maybe he was ill,

maybe he should go and see the doctor, but all that nonsense the old man had been spouting about power and time and monkeys — *monkeys, for goodness sake!* — was rubbish; the ramblings of some sort of dementia.

And yet, how could he have known about the boat in the fog? Gordon would have died before he would have told anyone about that. And something had happened in the room.

He became aware that as he stood there the green man had come and gone. He roused himself from his reverie and when the lights changed again he strode off.

It was a crisp autumn evening, and from George Street he could see the city strung with lights all the way to the Firth of Forth. He continued down the long slope towards home, turning along Northumberland Street with its tall houses. He always liked to glance in at the windows as he passed. Lots of folk never seemed to draw their curtains nowadays and he loved that snapshot of other people's lives. He looked in at kitchens, playrooms and sitting rooms, and some that were definitely drawing rooms. There were families eating or talking or watching television, and one household was having some sort of mock-Victorian evening, with a piano and costumes and everything.

He stopped dead, looking at the gaslights flickering in the drawing room, and the half a dozen men and women gathered round the piano.

This room wasn't like this!

He knew this street, played his spying game here two or three times a week. Everything about this room was wrong: the heavy curtains, the fire, the lights, even the paintings.

I will not panic.

He forced himself to close his eyes, counted to ten

and opened them. A man turned the music for the woman playing the piano. Gordon turned away and walked as fast as he could without running to the end of the street, and stood at the corner taking in cars and electric street lamps and normally dressed people.

You can only deny the truth for so long.

15. *Lies*

David was drowning in sleep. Every night now, he went to bed yawning ostentatiously as early as he reasonably could, and every morning he shut his ears to the sound of the alarm clock.

His days were increasingly focused on the moment when he could lie down in bed, switch off the light and launch himself willingly into the void of the dream.

He'd stopped being afraid of the Lightning Man; now he was little more than a distraction. He was there each night, sometimes on the lake, at other times already sitting on the shore. He would talk to David for a few minutes, mostly asking him questions for which he had no answers, about what it was like to live in a world in which time was so constrained. David replied as best he could, but all the time he was waiting for the sounds that told him his mother was approaching.

For the first few days he'd done little more than hold her, unable to stop the tears that slid down his face, but gradually he began to believe that she would be there the next night, and the next, and to talk to her. She asked questions as well, and these he had no trouble answering: they were about his dad and school and Kate and his other friends. She wanted to know about his life since she'd gone.

Time passed at a different rate in this dream world, where lightning coiled upwards like smoke from the man who sat silent, white teeth showing, watching and listening through the constant growl of his own thunder. He knew he slept for hours and never woke before the alarm forced him, but although he felt as though the dream had lasted all night, he never felt he'd had more than an hour or so with his mother.

It wasn't enough.

He found it hard to be enthusiastic about school, or football practice. Nothing seemed very important compared with the time he spent with his mother. He'd missed her so much and for so long, without realizing quite how deep the tear in his heart was. Now by some miracle he had her back every night.

He should have rushed to thank Mr Flowerdew for giving him the courage to look up, but something he couldn't put into words stopped him. He told no one, not even Kate, what was going on.

She had asked, of course, as soon as she saw him, the day after he decided to confront the dream; and for the first time ever, he had lied to her.

Not lied … It wasn't really a lie. He'd told her about the Lightning Man, and said he'd asked some questions and described the tendrils of lightning. He just hadn't mentioned his mum, and when Kate had asked him about the hiking boot, he shrugged and said quite smoothly, "I don't know. I didn't see it last night."

He kept to that story with Mr Flowerdew too, sticking as close to the truth as possible, but not mentioning his mother, admitting that the Lightning Man asked him questions, and that he was no longer afraid.

"So it is the Lightning King who troubles your dreams. I wondered when he would show himself. He is one of the Great Lords of Chaos. So is your dream visitor, Kate: Tethys the Water Witch. You have no need to fear them, as I've said. They can do you no harm, but they will try to persuade you to aid them instead of the Guardians."

"Don't worry," said Kate, "we're on your side. Aren't we, David?"

"Of course we are," David replied automatically. "How did things go with Gordon Syme?"

This was the reason for their latest meeting.

Mr Flowerdew — it was no good; they'd tried but couldn't call him John — made a face as though he'd bitten into something sour. "Not very well. I took him down to the round room and let him hear what you heard, then met him later and explained. He knows I've told him the truth, but he's trying to pretend to himself that it's all lies." He sighed, suddenly looking his age, whatever that was. "To be honest, I'm not quite sure what to do next about him. I think I will have to wait until he approaches me, but for once I am finding waiting a difficult task."

"We could try talking to him," suggested Kate.

"I don't think so ... he will see you only as children."

"Maybe we could convince him somehow."

"I don't see how you could."

"Anyway, there's no reason for us not to go to the museum, is there?"

"None at all — the more you know about it the better — but be careful what you say to Gordon Syme. We mustn't push him further away accidentally."

That had been a week ago, but they hadn't yet got round to visiting the museum. When Kate had suggested it, David said vaguely that he had stuff to do at home. He wasn't actually avoiding her, but he didn't seem interested in talking to her. In fact, he didn't seem interested in anything much except this mysterious *stuff*.

When she called round for him on Saturday morning for football practice, Alastair had to shake him awake and chivvy him out of his bed. He dressed with a bad grace and was sullen and off-form all morning. Kate was glad to say goodbye to him, irritated and worried at the same time.

Her concern for David made her restless and irritable, and for the rest of the day she found herself getting into fights with Ben over even less than usual. After one of them she shut herself in her room and took out Grandma Alice's gold necklace.

It was made of flattened links of gold, all identical and completely plain, except that when she turned it over she could see shapes engraved on some of the links which she swore had never been there before. They were very small, but quite clear, tiny picture shapes a bit like Egyptian hieroglyphs. How had they suddenly got there? They couldn't have been there before without her noticing, could they?

She kept going back to the necklace during the evening, half expecting the engraving to be gone, and the links to be blank once more, but they were still there. When her mother had come in to tell her it was bedtime, Kate had been terrified that she would take the necklace from her hand and see how it had changed, but she hadn't seemed to notice it.

Suddenly very tired, she turned off her lamp and squirmed down under the covers. She could hear the soft mutter of the television from the sitting room, otherwise it was quiet apart from an occasional car going past. She let her eyes close and stretched out yawning …

… and was standing once more in the cold desert.

This time, the woman who called herself Tethys was beside her at once, water slipping and dripping ceaselessly from her, her too-bright mouth curved in a smile. In the distance the wolves howled, but Kate couldn't see any sign of them.

"Kate, my dear. I have been impatient to see you

again. I have a present for you." She held out a hand. Dangling from finger and thumb was a magnificent gold bracelet, set with pearls and emeralds. "It is for you, my dear. Isn't it beautiful? Look." She moved it so that the light flashed off the polished surfaces. "It's for you. All I ask for in exchange is that plain little gold necklace of your grandmother's."

Kate moved slowly back. "No! You can't have that. It's mine. I'll never give it to you."

The bracelet of gold and pearls and emeralds swung before her eyes.

"Come, let me fasten it for you," said Tethys, her smile as sweet as ever. She held the bracelet in both hands and reached towards Kate's left wrist. Kate tried to move away, but something was behind her, rough hair against her legs, hot breath on her skin. She didn't dare turn to see it, and instead shouted desperately, "No! I don't want it. Leave me alone. I know who you are."

She sat up trembling in her own bed, her grandmother's necklace clutched so tight in her hand that the links had left an imprint.

By Sunday afternoon it was raining and the house was seething with bad temper.

"We need to get out somewhere," said Ruth.

"I don't want to go out in the rain," wailed Ben.

"Why don't we go to the museum?" Kate suggested.

"That's a good idea, Kate. What do you think, Ben? You can go and see the dinosaurs and you won't have to get wet."

"Good," said Ben emphatically.

The hall was crowded with people intent on finding a way to pass a wet Sunday afternoon. Damp tourists mingled with families, umbrellas dripped, and the fish spent their time speeding away from a hail of small change.

Ben pulled at his dad's hand. "Dinosaurs! I want to see the dinosaurs."

"All right, Ben, don't pull so hard, you'll have my arm off."

"Can I go round on my own for a bit?" asked Kate.

"I don't see why not. Don't go off with ..."

"I *know*, Mum."

"Sorry, love. We'll meet you in the café in half an hour, okay?"

"Forty-five minutes?"

"All right. Don't be late."

They separated and, walking quickly through the ground floor galleries, Kate began to look for Gordon.

No sign; but then, she didn't even know if he was here today. She paused to stare at the clock, looking especially hard at the little monkey in her golden clothes. Sometimes she had trouble believing that all this was really happening.

Should she go upstairs next, or into the new museum? She could wander round all afternoon and just keep missing him; and if she *did* find him, what exactly was she going to say?

She would worry about that if she found him.

She turned away from the clock towards the Information Desk, scanning faces.

The Information Desk ... Oh, she was such an idiot sometimes.

She hurried over. "Excuse me," she said to the woman on the desk, with her best smile. "Is Mr Syme working today? His first name's Gordon, I think."

"Let me check ... Do you know him, dear?"

"Oh no, not really, but my friend David and I were here for the sleepover a few weeks ago and had a really good time, and he was helping with it and I wanted to say hello."

Where on earth had all that come from? wondered Kate as it tumbled breathlessly out.

The woman smiled as she looked up from the form she was checking. "Yes, he's here." She looked at her watch. "He should just be coming back from his break. The best place to catch him is the room where the elephants are."

"Thank you."

Kate went to lie in wait among the elephants. Sure enough, a few minutes later, Gordon appeared round the corner, hands clasped behind his back, treading slowly. Kate pretended to be absorbed in the information board in front of her until he was almost level with her, then turned away from it as though lost in thought, and was able to literally bump into him.

"Oof!" he said as she stood on one of his feet and bounced off his stomach.

"Oh, I'm sorry." She shook her hair out of her eyes. "Oh hello, Mr Syme," she said as though she had just realized who he was. "I'm really sorry. I wasn't paying attention." She could see him trying to place her in his memory. "I'm Kate Dalgliesh ... from the sleepover. I was here with my friend David."

"Ah yes, I remember. Is he here today too?"

"No. I'm with my family. Mum and Dad and my little brother are up in the dinosaur bit."

"Say hello to your friend for me."

"I will." She paused. "Did you ever catch the rat or whatever it was that ate our biscuits?"

He looked suddenly wary. "No. No, we never did. It's gone anyway though. Must have sneaked out somehow. Don't you worry, it won't bother you if you come to another one."

"Oh, I'm not worried about that. It's just the dream."

"The dream?"

"Don't you remember? I disturbed you in the middle of the night by shouting out."

"Oh yes," he said, remembering vaguely.

"I keep having the same dream. I'm sure it's connected to being here. And my friend David — he's had really strange dreams since then too."

Gordon's face was pinched. "Have you told your parents?"

"No. Just Mr Flowerdew."

His eyes widened in shock, and she thought for a moment he would walk away from her. "How do you know him?" he said with a struggle.

"He was a friend of my grandma's. I've known him all my life. I know you didn't believe what he told ..."

"Kate! Kate! Mum says I can have a cake because I've been good."

Oh no — of all the moments! ...

"Please, talk to him again. He's told you the truth and he needs your help. We all do."

It was all there was time to say before Ben cannoned into her and her parents appeared at the other end of the gallery.

Would it be enough?

16. Cakes

"All right, I'll listen to you."

The old man had been in the Main Hall sitting on the whale rib chairs for an hour or so every afternoon for the last week. Gordon had avoided him until today, still wrestling with the thing in his head.

He looked up, keen-eyed, measuring. "What has changed your mind?"

"Partly what the wee girl said, and partly … I know something's not right. I haven't imagined all this."

"Will you come to my house?" He passed Gordon a small printed card. "The children will be there too. They have a part to play in this."

The boy opened the door to him before he'd had a chance to knock. What was his name again?

"Hello, Donald."

"It's David." He smiled as he said it. "Come in."

He remembered him now he saw him again, but he didn't look well. His face was pinched with dark smudges under his eyes; not the cheery child he'd met at the sleepover.

Gordon stepped into the hallway and looked round, taking in the great clock with its leisurely tick, the pictures and polished wood. It had been no surprise that the little printed card had led him to a fancy house in Bruntsfield.

David showed him into a big, bay-windowed room, crammed with books and pictures and an incongruous wide-screen TV. Gordon stared at it.

"Why is it," John Flowerdew said, coming into the room, "that everyone who comes to this house is surprised by the fact that I own a big television? I sometimes feel as if I've been caught breaking some sort of rule."

"You just don't look like the sort of person who has wide-screen," said Kate from behind him, catching Gordon's eye conspiratorially. "Hello, Mr Syme."

"Hello, Kate."

"Let's sit down," said Mr Flowerdew. Once they had done so, he went on, "How have things been in the museum?"

"Quiet," said Gordon, knowing he wasn't asking about visitor numbers or anything like that. "Whatever's been wandering about at night has stopped just now. It's just as well: people were starting to get a bit rattled. It's a wonder nobody blabbed to one of the papers about it all."

"If things continue to progress at their present rate it won't be long before something gets into print."

"I think I understand what you meant about all the power massed in the museum, and how it's begun to leak out. Is that what happened in the round room? Those voices?"

"Not exactly." Mr Flowerdew cast about for the right words. "Although the power is particularly strong in that room because of what it contains, on that occasion it was me acting as a channel for it, allowing the past to seep through. If the flow of time weakens further however, it will start to happen more and more of its own accord."

From the hall, the clock ticked into the silence.

"I didn't really let you explain what you thought was happening last time we spoke. I'm ready to hear it through this time."

As though this was a signal, Kate and David rose. "We've heard all this already," Kate explained. "We'll come back through in a while."

Before Gordon arrived they had been in the kitchen, baking cakes for the school fair — the reason for the visit as far as their parents were concerned. David checked the latest batch in the oven and took two out. They blew on them to cool them, then pulled off the tops and ate them.

"Perfect," said Kate. "Crisp top, raw middle. We should sell them this way."

"Doesn't work if they're cold though."

"No," she said regretfully. "Especially two days after they're made. Yuk!"

They laughed, everything normal for a brief moment.

"D'you reckon he'll agree to help us?" asked David, spreading icing.

"He turned up, didn't he? I can't see why he'd be here if he wasn't already convinced."

"That's not the same as agreeing to help though."

Kate sighed as she licked icing off a finger. "I know."

In the sitting room Gordon Syme sat, chin in hand, considering the unbelievable story he'd just been told. Any sane person would have walked out before now. Gordon decided that he was no longer sane, so he stayed ... and believed.

"Do the children really have to be part of this?" This was the part that troubled him most.

"It is essential. They each have a part to play that no one else can take, however much I wish that someone could. If we succeed they will come to no harm and if we fail they would be lost even if they had never been involved."

Gordon nodded slowly. If he believed the story, then it made sense. "And my part is to help you steal the Duddingston Hoard?"

"And to help me return it to its rightful place and time."

Gordon let out a short laugh and shook his head. "I'm sorry. I can't quite believe that I'm sitting here having this conversation. I'm seriously talking to you about helping steal an important exhibit so you can throw it in a loch?

"Oh well, when I'm brought to trial I'll have no trouble convincing them about diminished responsibility."

The door opened and the children came in with a plate of lopsided cakes. "Rejects," announced Kate. "Good enough to eat but not to sell."

Gordon watched them as they all sat eating, seeing them in a new light, though they still looked like two ordinary kids. They seemed to accept all this stuff as perfectly normal, though the boy looked a bit strained at times, when he thought no one's eyes were on him.

After two cakes, the girl said, "Have you decided?"

"Decided?"

"Will you help us?"

He took a breath. "Yes."

They all turned to Mr Flowerdew.

"Goodness," he said. "You look as if you expect me to make a speech or something. Let's finish our cakes in peace while we have the chance."

Gordon couldn't quite manage that. "When do we do whatever we're going to do?"

"That's a question I can't answer right away. I need to consult the other Guardians. We must attack the Lords of Chaos through many channels at once if this is to succeed. We have no chance if they can use anything like their full power against us here. I should think it will be four weeks or so before we can make our move.

"The Lords are bound to realize that a move against

them is coming. They will hurry to push open the door they have found here. More time slippages will happen, and more people will start to notice.

"We each have work to do in the meantime; you and I particularly, Gordon. We need to find out how to get the Hoard out of its case with as little fuss as possible.

"You know of course that the police will realize that someone on the museum staff must have been involved once they start investigating?"

Mr Flowerdew gave a smile that could only be described as gleeful. "If we are successful, the past will heal over with the Duddingston Hoard at the bottom of its loch and it will never have been discovered, so there will be no theft to investigate. The Hoard will never have been in the museum at all."

Gordon squeezed his eyes shut and shook his head, trying to make sense of that one.

"Neat," said Kate, who seemed to have no problem with it at all.

Maybe, thought Gordon, it wasn't the kids he should be worrying about after all …

17. Mum

As had become usual, David went to his room as early as he reasonably could that evening, telling his dad that he was going to revise in bed for his test tomorrow until he fell asleep.

"Don't tell me that's what they recommend nowadays?" said Alastair, raising an eyebrow.

"No, not exactly, but I thought maybe it'll stick better if it's the last thing I'm thinking about before I go to sleep."

"Well, I suppose it's worth a try. Don't work too late though."

"Don't worry, I won't. Goodnight."

"Sleep well."

So that he wouldn't have lied too blatantly, David did read over his work a couple of times before he switched off the light and readied himself to fall towards his dream ...

The Lightning King was already sitting on the shore. He'd made a little tower of pebbles in front of him, balanced in defiance of gravity. As usual, he seemed quite unconscious of the fronded lightning that flowed from his hands as he reached to place another one.

Instead of putting it on top of the pile, he lifted the whole tower on one finger, and slipped the new pebble in at the base, settling the others easily back down on it.

"How do you do that?" asked David, intrigued.

"You can see how I do it. You are watching me. It is simply a matter of finding the point of balance."

"I couldn't do that."

"True. But I have always been here. I have learned

the balance point of every stone on this shore." It should have sounded ridiculous, but David believed him without hesitation. "This time with your mother means a great deal to you, does it not?"

"Of course it does. She died when I was five. I've …' He stopped himself from saying more, but found he didn't need to.

"You've missed her for so long, every day, every night, and now you have her back. Of course it means a great deal … How long do you think these dreams will go on?"

David felt as though he'd been slapped in the face. "What do you mean?"

"Well, you cannot go on having the same dream every night for the rest of your life, can you? They must come to an end, but when will it be? Tonight? Next week? Next year?"

I … I don't know," he stammered. He had never thought of the possibility, had never *let* himself think of it. He couldn't lose his mother again, he just couldn't. "But you're making me have this dream. You can keep making me have it."

The Lightning King raised an elegant eyebrow. "You are mistaken. This dream is in your head, not mine. I have become a part of it, but I have no control over it."

"David!"

He turned to see his mother walking down the beach towards him and went to meet her, troubled and confused.

"Where do you come from?"

"What?"

"Before I see you here … Where are you?"

She frowned. "I don't know. I don't remember being anywhere but here. Does it really matter?"

"Yes! What if you don't come one night. How will I find you?"

She put a finger to his lips to quieten him. "Hush. I'll come to you."

"But what if I stop having this dream?" he persisted, his voice turning panicky.

"Then you'll wait for it to come back and I'll be here, waiting for you."

"But what if it *never* comes back? I don't want to lose you again, Mum. I can't."

She took his hand and pulled him down beside her and wrapped her arms around him until he stopped shaking, then she turned him to face her.

He looked at her, so solid and real, with her brown hair swinging to the shoulders of her red fleece, and her hazel eyes, with the little flecks of gold in them that he had always loved, looking steadily at him now.

"David, I am your mum *forever*; nothing can change that. I am here" — she touched his chest just over his heart — "and here," She held his head between her palms. "Always. *Always*. I couldn't be with you now if that wasn't true. Even if I'm not in your dreams, all you have to do is close your eyes and imagine me. Okay?"

"Okay," he said, in a voice that was little more than a whisper, then drew a deep breath and, from somewhere produced a smile.

"Now, tell me about your day."

This was how they usually began, before they branched off into whatever came to mind.

He didn't tell her everything.

He really didn't understand why himself, but he hadn't spoken to her at all about the Guardians and the Lords of Chaos and the clock. He had mentioned Mr Flowerdew once or twice, but only as the old man who had been a friend of Kate's grandma.

She accepted the truncated versions of his days without question, although to him it was terribly obvious he was leaving things out. Far stranger though was that she paid the Lightning King no heed at all, although they sometimes sat quite close to him on the shore.

It wasn't that she couldn't see him, for David had watched her eyes flicker onto him and then away again, and she wasn't exactly ignoring him — you could tell when one person was ignoring another on purpose — more that after that first glance he meant no more to her than any one of the pebbles on the shore.

David couldn't bring himself to ask her about it, afraid of anything that might disturb the dreams.

"My day? Kate and I made some cakes for the school fair on Saturday and ..."

The Lightning King was out on the water the next night, idly casting ropes of lightning towards the violet horizon. "I have thought about what you said about the dreams ending," he said.

David felt as though someone was squeezing his chest in a giant fist. "Yes?"

The King turned and walked to the edge of the lake. "I could help."

David's heart leapt. "But how? You said you don't control the dreams."

"I don't. I am not talking about the dreams. You could have your mother back all the time; not just when you're asleep."

"I can't. Don't you understand? She's dead."

"I know that. And she will stay dead if you do what John Flowerdew and his allies wish. Dead forever." He stopped, head cocked to one side, watching David's face, waiting for him to realize the import of what he had not said.

After an age, David spoke. "What happens if I don't do it?"

"Then time will be freed from its constraints, and the past — all the past — will be here in the present, and your mother will be here, alive, all the time."

David felt as though he had forgotten how to breathe as he worked to force air in and out of his lungs. He found that he was on his knees on the pebbles, but he couldn't remember kneeling. The King watched him with detached interest, as though he was a struggling insect.

His breathing grew easier. "If you win, my mum's alive?" he asked, fearful of the answer.

The King nodded silently and walked off out across the water again. David struggled to his feet and stared after him. He heard the crunch of pebbles under a hiking boot and turned to greet his mother.

Kate tried to wake up, but it was no good; the dream had her, and whichever way she turned Tethys stood before her, barely an arm's length away, smiling her hungry smile, her wolves beside her. In her wet hands she held a necklace of gold and shimmering stones, whose colours shifted and rippled like the surface of the sea. "Is it not beautiful?"

"Go away! I won't give you my necklace."

"But Kate, it is such a small thing to ask for all that I could give in return. We could be like sisters, you and I. Join me in my power … just this one, small thing."

"No!"

Tethys' face hardened. "Then I shall give you a demonstration of the power you would cast aside. I will call up a piece of the past … something you will heed."

She closed her eyes, and a wind roared out of the

desert, roared out of nowhere, swirling around them. Her eyes flew open and held Kate's own.

"Wake!"

Kate sat up with a gasp in bed, alone, of course. She had taken to sleeping with the necklace in its box under her pillow, and felt for it now, to check it was safe. As she did so, there was a soft knock on the door, and her mother's voice.

"Kate love, are you all right?" The door opened and she saw her mother as an indistinct silhouette in the doorway. "I heard you yelling. Did you have a bad dream?"

"Sorry, I didn't realize I'd made a noise. I'm fine."

Her mother came a little further into the room. "Well, if you're sure ..." Without warning she was interrupted by a sound from the street: the sound of howling. Kate froze in horror, eyes wide as her mother crossed to the window and lifted a curtain to look out, apparently unconcerned. "Goodness, what a noise those dogs are making. I wonder who they belong to? I don't recognize them. You'd almost think they were wolves — they even sound like them. Anyway, they've run off up the hill now.' She twitched the curtain back into place and turned to leave. "Ugh, what's that? The floor's all wet." She turned on the light, and squinting half-blinded, Kate saw a great dark patch on the carpet near the foot of the bed and felt cold with fear.

"Where did this come from?" Her mother looked up at the ceiling. "Kate?"

As she opened her mouth to say something, there was a low growling noise from somewhere outside. It grew steadily louder, until the room seemed to shake and her window rattled in its frame. In the next bedroom she heard Ben yell in fright and start to cry.

18. *Tremors*

Next morning, as they set up their stall at the school fair, much of the talk was of the disturbance that had woken them all during the night. The local news had been full of it this morning — *Earth Tremor Shakes City* — but actual facts were in short supply. Everyone had their own theory.

"I bet it was a gas explosion," said Karin Griffiths.

"No, that's too boring," George Marshall said decisively. "I think Arthur's Seat's about to erupt. This is only the beginning."

"I bet they've been testing a secret weapon underground and it's gone wrong." George's brother Sam had stopped on his way past to join in.

"What are you all talking about?" asked David, coming in late.

"The earth tremor, of course."

"What earth tremor?"

"In Holyrood Park, last night. You must have felt it," said Kate. "I did, and you live nearer to it than I do."

"I never noticed a thing."

"What about your dad?"

"Dunno. He was still asleep when I left."

"Honestly, David, you're unbelievable sometimes. You don't even look interested."

"I am, I am; I'm not properly awake yet, that's all. When did you say it happened?"

"About three o'clock this morning."

"Have buildings collapsed and everything?"

The others looked a bit crestfallen.

"No. Just some cracked walls and broken windows."

As they spoke they had been unrolling paper tablecloths over a couple of classroom tables to make them look hygienic.

"Right. Let's arrange the cakes," said Karin, ever practical.

By ten o'clock they'd discussed every possible cause of the tremor, and rearranged the cakes for the third time. They had to admit there was nothing more they could do until the fair opened at eleven, so they went back to Kate's house for a quick snack.

In the kitchen, they fiddled with the radio until it picked up a local station, then waited for a news bulletin.

"... Scientists are urgently seeking an explanation for the series of earth tremors that shook Edinburgh during the night. The tremors were felt over a wide area of the city, but were strongest in and around Holyrood Park. Some nearby houses suffered minor structural damage and have been evacuated as a precaution.

"The Edinburgh Seismic Survey recorded the event, which measured 5.1 on the Richter Scale, making it the strongest tremor ever recorded anywhere in the United Kingdom. Although geologists have known for years that the Central Belt used to be a hot spot for earthquakes and volcanic eruptions, there has been virtually no seismic activity in the region for millions of years, and experts have admitted that this was completely unexpected ..."

Kate went cold all over. Millions of years ... *I will call up a piece of the past*. What if the past was leaking through, called up by Tethys?

She kicked David under the table, motioned for him to follow her out of the room, and once they were safely in the hall, she told him about the previous night's dream. "What do you think?" she asked. "It can't just be a coincidence, can it? I wonder if Mr Flowerdew knows?"

"Of course he will; it sounds as though I'm the only person in Edinburgh who didn't feel it."

"Mmmn ... I still can't understand how it could wake us down here, but not you."

David shrugged. "I suppose I must just have been in a deep sleep."

"Are you still having your dream? You haven't mentioned it for a while."

"Yeah, but it doesn't worry me like it used to. It was just like he said — I faced up to it and it stopped being frightening."

"Hey, you two, stop whispering," yelled George, coming out of the kitchen.

"We'd better go back now."

Kate and David managed to lag behind on the way so that they could carry on their conversation.

"If we are right about the tremor, it must be a bad sign that so may people felt it, mustn't it? I mean, it's become real now. The other things that have happened have sort of faded away or only affected a few people.

"This must mean the Lords of Chaos are getting stronger, and that means we'll have to do something soon. Oh David, what's happening to us?"

They had stopped walking and stood now staring at each other, both truly frightened at last.

He looks ill, thought Kate. *He's so pale. Do I look like that? What's wrong with him?*

After they'd cleared up the remains of their stall, which had been stripped bare of cakes — even the really grotty ones — in just over an hour, Kate and David walked along to the newsagent's. They had to wait while the shopkeeper hustled a teenage girl — homeless by the look of her baggy, tatty clothes — out of the shop before they could buy a copy of *The Edinburgh Evening News*.

The earth tremor was the main story.

They stood in the street heedless of other people, scanning the page, looking for clues, hoping that there would be something to explain it that would fix it firmly in the normal present day, but the article had the opposite effect.

Scientists were baffled. The seismic traces were the sort that would have been typical in the Central Region when its great chain of volcanoes had been active, millions of years before. No one could explain why this had happened now.

"Oh no," said Kate. "It's starting to come apart, isn't it?"

"Sounds like it," said David absently, still reading.

They stopped at a call box to telephone Mr Flowerdew and arranged to meet in Luca's café that afternoon. He was hopeful that Gordon would be there too. He sounded grim.

"Time, as we understand it, is running short. The Lords of Chaos are gathering their strength. Be on your guard."

They sat at a purple table tucked into a corner and ordered delicious ice creams that they didn't feel like eating. Gordon was already there when they arrived, looking ill at ease and suddenly much younger without his museum uniform. Mr Flowerdew arrived a few minutes later, looking flustered; something they had never seen before.

"I'm afraid there is no doubt," he said, "that this tremor is what we feared: evidence of a rip in time. We have no choice but to act in the next few days, or it will be too late. I have been in contact with some of the other Guardians. They are as well prepared as they can be to draw some of the Lords away from this battle-ground to fight them elsewhere.

"Gordon; how soon can you get the keys that we need to get in to the Hoard?"

"I'm not on until Tuesday morning. I'll get all the information then, and arrange to swap a night duty with someone."

"How easy will that be?"

He gave a small smile. "That's the one bit that will be no problem at all. What night do you want?"

"The longer we delay, the more dangerous things will become. I can be ready for Wednesday."

"Right. I'll see to that."

"Kate, David ..." Mr Flowerdew looked at them, searching for words. "The need to act has come sooner than I hoped. I am sorry, but there is no help for it. Be dressed and ready at midnight on Wednesday. Watch from a window until you see my car, then come out quickly."

"But what if someone sees one of us waiting? They'll never let us go out with you at that time."

"Don't worry about that. I can make sure that they sleep soundly throughout that night, and won't know you've gone. If everything goes well, you'll be back in your beds in a couple of hours, and they'll never know anything has happened."

"It's going to be difficult to do what you need to in the Main Hall without one of the lads walking in on it," said Gordon.

"That too is something I should be able to control. As Guardians, we have some power over time. When we are in the museum we will be in our own bubble of time, and no one should be aware of us. I wish there was another way though — any interference with the flow of time weakens it; and that makes it easier for Chaos to disrupt it completely."

"What will happen to us," said Kate, in a voice that sounded very small, "if things go wrong? Will we die?"

Mr Flowerdew leaned across the table and grasped her hand briefly and sighed. "No, my dear. If Chaos wins, you can never die, for there will be no future. The flow of time will stop; there will only be the past and the present, swirling together with no end. I am glad that you cannot truly imagine it, for it is terrible beyond words."

The past and the present, swirling together with no end. David heard the words and a picture formed in his mind of his mum back with him and his dad again. They would always be together, and all that he had to do was ...

"What exactly do we do?" he heard himself ask.

"Gordon, can you let us in at the wheelchair entrance at the rear of the building?"

Gordon nodded. "Shouldn't be a problem. That's the best place."

"Once we are inside we will go together to the Main Hall, and Gordon and I will keep watch while the two of you chain the monkey. Let me see the necklace, Kate."

She pulled the little box out of the pocket of her fleece and handed it to him.

"It's changed," she said.

He took it out and studied it closely.

"Yes," he said. "Power calls to power. These signs have stayed hidden for many years, but now the chain shows its true nature."

He showed her how to pull the fine chain back

through the fastening ring at each end to make a double loop.

"Once you have it ready like this," he said, "you must wait for the monkey to let go of the handle."

"What?" asked David, incredulous.

"But you said it didn't move," protested Kate.

"And that was true. But the forces of Chaos will be focused on us, and that will bring the power to such a pitch that she will be able to free herself physically from the mechanism. That is the moment — the *only* moment — at which we can trap her.

"As soon as her paws come off the handle you must slip one of the loops over it and the other over her left paw, then force both paws onto the handle again so that the right one stops the chain slipping off. Do you see?"

They nodded.

"As soon as you have the necklace on her and return her hand to the handle the power we face should diminish. Then Gordon and I will take the hoard from its case and together we will return it to the bottom of Duddingston Loch. And then we shall see if it is enough."

"Why can't *you* put the necklace on?" asked Kate.

"When it was made it was *tuned* to your grandmother. Later, when you two were born, it was retuned to the pair of you. Neither one of you can use it on your own; only together can you activate its binding power. In my hands, or Gordon's or anyone else's, it is just a piece of jewellery; in yours it becomes a weapon."

He pushed the box back across the table to Kate, and she put it back into her pocket in silence.

"'There is little more that we can do to prepare. It is probably best if we do not meet again before Wednesday night. Gordon, telephone me once you have been to work. We need to know if there is any reason why we cannot act on Wednesday night."

Gordon nodded.

"I know I am asking a great deal of each of you. I wish it was not necessary. Things may get worse quickly now, and the Lords will redouble their efforts to stop us. Be on your guard."

19. Finis

Andrew Nixon settled down in front of the fire with Sir Edmund Shackleton's biography.

Life had improved, he had to admit it. That stupid hallucination incident had let him see what a threadbare existence he led. His sister had talked good sense about how he needed to take better care of himself and had persuaded him to hire the housekeeper he had talked about for so long.

He'd seen her giving the birds and animals some sidelong glances as he showed her over the house during the interview, and for a while he had thought she might not turn up, but she had started on Monday, having explained proudly to her friends that she was going to work for an eccentric gentleman who kept a house full of dead beasts, and even after only two days the difference was obvious. The house was bright and clean and smelled of polish. The fire was lit when he came home and there was a meal waiting for him in a slow oven. He'd cut back on the hours he worked as well, and started going for walks — he knew he didn't take enough exercise. He didn't exactly feel like a whole new man, but the beginnings of one at least.

In fact, he thought, he might just take a turn along the shore now — it was a lovely winter evening — and drop into the Cramond Inn on the way back for a sociable whisky.

He marked the place in his book, put the guard in front of the fire and went downstairs. He checked in his jacket pocket to make sure he had his keys and let himself out.

It was a crisp, clear evening with a full moon burning

cold above the trees. He walked past the building site without his heart rate even rising and strolled along the sea front looking at the jumbled necklaces of light, which marked the town centre. Away ahead on the beach, he could just make out a couple throwing sticks for their dog, which dashed in and out of the surf yelping with pleasure.

As he watched, the lights winked out.

A power cut. Must be a big one: there were no lights anywhere ahead. He imagined the chaos there would be in town; traffic lights out, pubs, cinemas and houses plunged into unexpected darkness, the scramble for torches and candles.

He turned back towards the village. There were no lights here either unless you counted the moonlight. He'd been looking forward to a drink in front of the pub fire, but now he may as well just go home. He started for the Tower House.

The lack of any light other than the moon was disorienting. He couldn't make out quite where he was in relation to his home. He saw a light ahead and made for it, to get his bearings. He was quite close before he realized it was a fire, and even then it was a few seconds before his brain caught up with his body and stopped him walking towards it.

But by then, it was already too late. He pressed a hand over his mouth to stop himself screaming as he stared in horror at the impossible Roman camp around him. His legs shook so badly he thought he would fall. He tried to run, even to walk, but he couldn't move, and it was with a curious sense of detachment that he watched one of the soldiers jump to his feet, sending the knucklebones flying, as he noticed him.

Four of them were on their feet now, hands making the sign against evil as they reached for their swords.

They came at him moving as though in slow motion and yet were upon him with terrible swiftness. As they came, Andrew Nixon thought he saw a figure behind them, dressed in black rags, that blew in a wind that wasn't there; smiling as he watched.

The swords rose and fell, rose and fell, then were still.

20. *The Blood Moon*

Kate sat by her bedroom window, fully dressed but shivering, staring out into a world white with fog. It was ten to midnight on Wednesday. The necklace lay coiled in its box in her pocket, her hand wrapped around it.

The last three days had passed in a sort of numb daze, about which she could remember almost nothing. She knew she must have gone to school, eaten meals with her family, talked to people, but she could recall no detail at all. The only thing she could remember clearly was the blank, sick look in David's eyes; much like her own, she supposed.

She had noticed the increasing number of strange local news stories: a dog, which looked identical to the statue of Greyfriars Bobby, had taken up residence in Greyfriars Kirkyard; residents in a city centre street swore their milk had been delivered by a horse-drawn cart; tours of the tunnels under the Royal Mile had been suspended after eighteen people on five different tours had to be brought out, almost hysterical, claiming to have seen the ghosts of men and women pointing at them and screaming in fear; an elusive group of new age travellers were believed to have set up some sort of Bronze-Age-style camp somewhere in Holyrood Park, but the authorities couldn't find them; and the soldiers garrisoned at the Castle were being disturbed night after night by sounds of shouting and artillery bombardment that no one could explain.

To Kate and David, it made dreadful sense.

She started as something slipped across the patch of indistinct yellow light from the street lamp: it had looked like a large rangy dog. She held her breath, waiting for howling, but the night stayed quiet.

From his window, at exactly the same time, David watched mist tracking across the face of the full moon, dimming its light. He didn't know how he felt — not excited, not fearful — it was as though he was a machine on which someone had pressed the pause button.

He hadn't been to sleep. It was the first night he'd missed seeing his mother since the dreams began. He wondered if she was waiting on the shore. Was she there if he wasn't?

A car stopped outside and he recognized it as Mr Flowerdew's. He went out of his room and bent to scratch Tiger under the chin as he passed. The cat purred deep in his chest. As quietly as he could, David unlocked the door and pulled it shut behind him.

A few seconds later he was in the back of the car, where Kate already sat, pale and tense. Mr Flowerdew nodded in greeting, but didn't speak. Fog swirled cold around the car, bouncing the light from the headlamps back at them. They set off slowly.

Although there wasn't very much traffic on the roads, it seemed to take forever to reach the museum. The fog swirled about them erratically, making it difficult to judge distances and the speeds of the few other cars that were about.

By the time they reached the Meadows it seemed they were moving hardly faster than walking pace, and the fog clung malevolently to the car in great wet sheets. In the back seat, the children edged closer to each other without realizing, keeping as far away from it as possible.

Kate found her voice. "Is this just ordinary fog?"

"No indeed," said Mr Flowerdew. "It is a fog such as no one in Edinburgh has ever seen. The Lords are trying to delay us."

Whether it was coincidence, they never knew, but as he spoke, the fog rolled back from the car for a moment and they caught a glimpse of the trees and paths of the Meadows and above them a cloud-pocked sky and the full moon.

Kate let out a gasp, heard the others exclaim.

The moon was blood red.

"What is it?" David managed to ask. "What's happened to the moon?"

"It is an eclipse — but it should not be happening now. We must hurry; they are close to breaking through."

Even as he spoke however, the fog closed in again, hiding the disfigured moon and forcing them to slow down again.

David clutched at Kate's arm. "Look!"

On one side of them, where there should have been the level grass of the Meadows, there was a rippling body of water, and on the other, so close that twigs scraped the windows of the car, the edge of a dense tract of forest.

"What's happening?"

Mr Flowerdew kept his eyes on the non-existent road as he replied, "This is what used to be here hundreds of years ago. The past is breaking loose." Around them, the fog had closed in again.

They crawled on, drawing closer to the incongruously visible traffic lights. As they reached them, the fog thinned once more to show daylight, and a crowded huddle of huts and tents where a moment ago there had been water. Everywhere people sat or lay, thin and ragged, indifferent to their surroundings. The stench from the camp penetrated the car; a terrible smell of rotting bodies, not yet dead.

Mr Flowerdew drew in his breath sharply and increased the car's speed. "A plague camp," he said, almost to himself. "I had hoped never to see anything like that again."

A woman looked up and seemed to see them properly for the first time, and pointing, began to scream. Others followed her glance, and the camp erupted like a kicked anthill. Even as it did so however, it flickered and disappeared. It was night again, and everything around them, including the moon, looked as it should.

"They are distracted. Now we have a chance."

He threw the car around the corner and they sped through the quiet streets until they pulled up a few minutes later at the top of the lane that ran up one side of the museum.

The fog settled back thicker than ever as though someone had thrown a blanket over them. They held hands as they moved through it towards the door where Gordon should be waiting.

Mr Flowerdew knocked sharply three times. It opened immediately and Gordon nodded them in silently. He closed the door, holding the fog at bay, and they relaxed a little in the faintly-lit corridor that lay behind it.

"Is everything ready?"

Gordon nodded. "I've got the keys. How was it, getting here?"

"More difficult than I had hoped. Is there somewhere that we can talk for a moment?"

"In here." He opened the door to a room that was little more than a store cupboard and switched on the light.

"The power is nearing its zenith. We don't have much time. Gordon — you and I must go straight to the Hoard. David, Kate; you know what to do. We cannot be with you while you do it — time is too short."

"But ..."

"You *can* do this. Have faith in yourselves." A wisp of fog crept under the door. "We must go now, or there will be no more time."

Gordon led them down an unfamiliar corridor, across a lecture theatre and then through the dark, silent café out into the Main Hall. A light glowed at the Information Desk where Sandy sat.

Gordon stopped.

"He can't see us. He will not know anything is happening," said Mr Flowerdew. "Come, we must hurry." He turned to the children. "Don't be afraid. You know what to do." And they went off down the hall, past the oblivious Sandy.

Kate and David looked at each other, and then at the clock, a huge, brooding presence. Against the glass of the roof and windows the fog flattened itself, seeking entrance. Gordon and Mr Flowerdew were already lost to sight in the gloom at the far end of the hall.

Kate took a shaky breath and started towards the clock, David hanging back a little. They reached the thick brown rope that kept the public at a distance from it during the day and paused.

In the dim and patchy light only some of the clock's detail was visible, so that while the great curved mirror shone like a ghostly eye, the top of the tower with its agonized figures was no more that an indistinct bulk rearing up towards the night sky.

The monkey's golden ornaments gleamed softly, utterly still. Kate stepped over the rope and edged towards her, fear rising in her throat. "David, come on!" she hissed.

Reluctantly he moved to follow her.

Cautiously, Kate stretched out a hand and touched the monkey's wooden paw with one fingertip. Nothing happened. The paw was indeed wood, lifeless as it should be.

More boldly, she moved her hand up and down the monkey's arm, then tried to lift her paws from the handle. There was no movement at all as she threaded one end of the necklace in a loop around its wrist and got the other end ready to go round the handle. Finished, she took a step back, and bumped into David.

"Kate, look." His voice sounded odd.

She turned around and froze. Not five metres away stood Tethys, streaming water that drained away into the marble floor. The wolves circled her restlessly as though waiting for her to release them. Her smile was gone, and in its place was a look of ferocious anger. "Kate," she said in a commanding voice, "stop this now. You do not understand what you are doing. Give me the necklace."

"No! Go away and leave us alone!"

David watched the exchange, wide-eyed. How could Kate defy this terrible woman?

There was a laugh from further down the hallway, and a low growl of thunder. The Lightning King drifted nonchalantly a little above the floor, his robes blowing in the non-existent wind. Everything about him — his robes, his skin, his hair — was filigreed with lightning, crawling over him like tiny snakes.

"David, who is he?"

"The Lightning King — the man from my dream."

He heard Kate whimper, and remembered how frightened he had been of the King at first.

"It's all right. He won't hurt us."

"He is right. I have no desire to hurt you."

Lightning flew up from his hand, and a wolf howled,

and they heard glass break far above them, but he made no move to come closer to them. Tethys too kept her distance.

Somehow, Kate made herself turn back towards the monkey, and what she saw shocked her anew.

All the golden ornaments were still in place and the monkey still gripped the handle tightly, motionless; but where there had been wood, now there was flesh, and instead of paint, there was hair.

"David!" She tugged urgently at his sleeve. "The monkey's changing. This is when we have to do it. *David*!"

He hung back, watching the King. There was more lightning, and he heard another pane of glass shatter high in the roof. He could imagine the fog creeping in.

Kate had the end of the necklace in her hand, looped and ready as she watched the monkey blink as though in slow motion. Tethys called out something in words that Kate didn't understand and the monkey turned its head towards her, teeth bared. She realized that her wrist was constrained and shook her arm, growling as Kate held tight to the end.

"David! Help me!"

But David was watching the wolves padding towards them on silent paws, fangs showing.

The monkey lifted her paws off the handle and made to claw at Kate's eyes, snarling. She screamed, but held tight to the necklace, and David, like someone waking from a trance, forced his gaze away from the wolves, and rushed to help her.

He grabbed the monkey's wrists and forced them back towards the handle as she twisted and bit at them. Thunder rolled around them and lightning flashed and Tethys' shouts reached a crescendo as Kate managed to slip the loop of gold over the handle.

"Now!"

They both brought their weight to bear on the monkey's arms as she screeched in fury. Down and down they pressed and as her paws touched the handle, Kate saw from the corner of her eye one of the wolves gather itself to spring, and in the same moment the monkey changed, no longer flesh and angry blood, but wood and paint again. Around her wrist and around the handle looped the subtle golden manacle that would keep her tied to the clock. Even as they watched, it seemed to melt away into the wood.

Around them, there was a profound silence. The wolves were gone. As Kate watched, Tethys shimmered and dissolved like a reflection in rippled water.

Further away, the Lightning King too was growing indistinct, merging into the fog that had poured through the broken panes of glass. His blue eyes were fixed on David.

"You have another chance," he said, and was gone.

Kate and David stood shakily, panting as if after a race.

"What did he mean?" she managed to ask.

"I don't know." The lie came out glibly, disguising the turmoil of his emotions. He should have stopped Kate; he had meant to, but then when the monkey was clawing at her he'd acted without thinking, and by the time he'd realized what he was doing it was too late.

But it was all right; the King had said he had another chance. What it was he didn't know, but he would make no mistake next time. He couldn't; everything depended on getting it right.

They stepped back over the rope. Fog trickled in from the roof, pooling on the floor here and there. Moving round it, they set off to find Gordon and Mr Flowerdew.

21. Duddingston

As they made their way down to the round chamber at the root of the museum, Gordon and Mr Flowerdew did not speak. The air brushed against them heavily, as though trying to slow them down, and they seemed to move with painful slowness towards their destination.

It was even worse when they got there. The air smelled as it does during a storm, crackling with unseen electricity, and buzzing with angry, indistinct voices.

Gordon had disabled a security camera in the hall with the striding figures, and now all there was to do was unlock the display case with the key he had pocketed earlier that day.

At the threshold of the room Mr Flowerdew put a hand on his shoulder to stop him for a moment. "The presences in this room are waking. I will do what I can to hold them at bay. Open the case and put all the pieces of the Hoard in the bag. Do not stop, whatever seems to be happening."

Gordon threw him a rather wild-eyed look, but went to the cabinet without comment.

Mr Flowerdew stood in the centre of the room, eyes half-closed, face tilted towards the ceiling.

Gordon unlocked the cabinet and slid the door open.

There was a sound that was not quite a human voice, not quite singing. It made the hackles rise on the back of Gordon's neck as its keening noise grew, rising higher and higher. He glanced round at Mr Flowerdew, standing erect in the centre of the room. The old man hadn't moved, his face turned to the ceiling, arms by his side.

Gordon forced himself to turn back to the case and with clumsy fingers began to lift the hoard of broken weapons into an open holdall.

Angry voices swooped about him like birds trying to strike at his head, and unconsciously he hunched lower as he transferred the fragile pieces of metal.

Above everything rose the dreadful inhuman keening.

Gordon found he was panting for breath, though his movements seemed slow as a swimmer's.

As he put the last of the weapons in the bag there was a new sound, as if something heavy was breaking through twigs and branches.

"Hurry! I cannot hold them."

The old man's face was running with sweat. From across the room Gordon could see him trembling with exertion. He forced himself to lift the bag and walk towards him.

Just as he thought the noise was so loud that the walls must start to crumble, everything stopped.

The absence of sound was a physical relief that brought him momentarily to a halt before he lurched forward again to offer his arm to the old man, who looked on the verge of collapse.

"Thank you," he said shakily. "The children must have succeeded. They have won us a little respite, but we must leave this place." They left the circular chamber on uncertain legs.

Gordon looked back once and suppressed a cry. The ancient carved figure from Ballachulish lay half out of its case in a welter of broken glass and twigs.

By the time they reached the children in the Main Hall, they had regained some of their composure. The children were wide-eyed with fear, but calm. Fog poured in through the broken roof panes, pooling on the floor and sending out tendrils. Gordon led them back a different way so that they could avoid it completely.

They opened the door on a world run mad.

Around them, buildings flickered in and out of existence, and the light shifted and changed constantly. At one moment the blood moon stood in the sky; at the next, the sun. Trees appeared and disappeared around them. Only Mr Flowerdew's car remained a constant among the bewildering maelstrom.

They rushed to its illusory safety and shut themselves in, speechless at what they could see happening outside.

"Time is unravelling."

Mr Flowerdew started the car, which sat, at the moment, on a windswept moor, and it moved off, bouncing slowly over the uneven ground. Gordon sat forward, gripping the dashboard, peering out. Kate and David huddled in the back seat, speechless.

Buildings and roads flickered around them. It was night-time; gaslights, a horse-drawn cab. The horse shied at the unfamiliar mechanical horror bearing down on it and the cabbie yelled with fear, jumped down and took to his heels.

A forest now, the trees close enough to touch, but somehow a clear path always opening just in front of them. Dappled light and soft rain.

The light thickened to the colour of honey and they saw men stripped to the waist building a great wall of dark stone.

Fog again, their own time returned for a few moments, and they found themselves by Holyrood Palace, at the entrance to the great park.

David glanced at Kate, saw her face was glazed with fear, wondered what his own looked like.

It'll be all right, he thought. *I'll stop them and Mum will come back forever and everything will be all right.*

Now that they were in the park, although the sky changed every few seconds, the shifts in the landscape around them were less marked. Holyrood Park had stood virtually unchanged for thousands of years, since the hill tribes abandoned it.

The road disappeared again, and Mr Flowerdew slowed the car to negotiate a narrow track across a steep slope.

"Why does the car stay the same?" asked Gordon, breathlessly.

"Because I force it to remain," said Mr Flowerdew shortly, his face gaunt with strain.

They could see Duddingston Loch now, glimmering ahead and to the right of them. The blood moon shone in the sky again, but it was not the sky of their own time. The loch was much bigger than it should have been, and there was no church at its far end, no building anywhere in fact.

The track petered out, and Mr Flowerdew stopped the car. "These will be the hardest moments. Be brave and we may still succeed."

To leave the tiny measure of safety provided by the car was almost more than they could bear, but somehow they did it, Gordon picking up the bag of broken weapons and helping the children out.

"This way." Mr Flowerdew led them through hip-high grass down towards the loch. There was just enough light to see that at this end it extended into a narrow tongue of silvery water.

Gordon put down the bag a little way from the edge and unzipped it.

"What the …?"

He reached into the bag and pulled out a spearhead,

whole and gleaming; nothing like the fragile and corroded fragments he had taken from the museum.

"In this time the weapons are newly forged," said Mr Flowerdew by way of explanation. "Now we must each return something to the water."

He went first, scooping up blades and spearheads. He walked to the water's edge and threw them, one by one, as far as he could out into the loch. They flew in silvery arcs against the sky.

As he turned back to the others, Gordon called, "Over there, look."

On the other side of the inlet stood three men, dressed in skins and carrying spears and bows. The two groups stood motionless watching each other for a few seconds, then the men melted away into the undergrowth.

"Pay them no heed. We are in their time. It was men such as them who left the Hoard here in the first place. Come along ... hurry!"

Gordon went next, then came back to where the bag lay to help the children.

As Kate waited her turn she looked around. "What's that? What's happening?"

In the sky on the other side of the loch, lightning flashed and a glow of golden light spread up from the ground to meet it.

"It is the battle for which the weapons were made. Quickly. This must be done now."

Kate turned and took a bone-handled knife and some spearheads from Gordon. The knife began to glow with the same golden light that was leaping in the sky.

"What should I do?"

A wind had suddenly risen from nowhere and Mr Flowerdew had to shout.

"Throw them in. Now!"

She flung them and watched the glow disappear beneath the dark waters of the loch.

"It's your turn, David," said Gordon.

He hesitated, then dug his hand into the bag and pulled out the last weapon, a golden, glowing sword. It was cool under his fingertips, though it looked as though it should have burned.

"Now comes the moment when you must decide, David."

He looked up sharply, into the eyes of the Lightning King, barely five metres away, in the opposite direction from the loch. He was drenched in lightning and now it ran down, not up, pooling around his feet, to form a miniature silver lake.

"Throw the sword in here, and your mother can be with you for ever."

Beside him, Gordon stood frozen. At the loch side, Kate and Mr Flowerdew stood, appalled.

Kate found her voice first. "David! Quick! Throw the sword in the loch."

He didn't move.

Mr Flowerdew and the Lightning King locked gazes.

"You are an old man, Guardian. A weak old man," said the King, smiling his wolf's smile. "And you have failed."

With an obvious effort, Mr Flowerdew turned his eyes to David. "David, please, think about the things I told you. Think of what you have seen tonight. Would you have this happen to your world?"

"I'll get my mum back."

He heard Kate gasp. "But she's *dead*, David."

"Not if time comes apart. She'll come back. We'll be together forever."

The King spoke again. "It is time. Throw the sword to me. See, here is your mother."

He lifted his head and saw his mother, her red fleece bright even in the ruddy moonlight, walking down through the grass towards him. He swung his arm back.

"Wait, David!"

He lowered his arm again and waited for her to reach him.

She was crying.

"Don't cry, Mum. It'll be all right, you'll see. In a minute it'll be all right and you'll be back with me and Dad forever."

Her hand was on his arm, preventing him from throwing the glowing sword. "No, David. Throw it in the loch. You mustn't do this."

"What?" he shouted in disbelief. "You don't understand. If I throw it in the loch you stay dead. If I throw it into the lightning, you won't be dead anymore."

"No, David."

He had never seen her look so sad.

"I won't be dead anymore and I'll be here somewhere like this, but I'll be here every day that I was ill as well, and you and Dad will have to go through it over and over again … for ever. Don't do that to us. Let me go."

It was as though she had asked him to tear out his own heart. "No. I can't. Don't ask me to do that."

"You can. Remember, I told you before: I am here," — she touched his heart — "and here," — his head — "always. Close your eyes and I'll be there. You don't need this. Be brave. You know what you must do."

"No." He whispered, his head against her chest, wrapped in her dear arms. She was asking him never to stand like this again. "I can't."

She tilted his head with her hands so he had to look her in the eyes. "You can. Come on, I'll walk down to the water's edge with you."

She took his free hand and led him, no longer protesting, to the shore of the loch, paying no heed to Kate or Mr Flowerdew as she passed them.

Through tears she smiled and bent to kiss him for the last time. “I’m so proud of you. My brave son.”

Then she turned him to face the water and stood behind him as he hurled the final piece of the Hoard in a golden arc into Duddingston Loch, and when he turned back she was gone.

He fell to his knees with a sob.

The ground under him shuddered as the Lightning King gave a great cry of rage and the silver pool about his feet began to boil. Around him, Kate saw figures flicker in and out of time: Tethys and others whom she did not recognize, some human-looking, others horned or animal-headed, called from whatever other battles they had been fighting elsewhere, too late to help in this one. Howls and shouts split the air. The King began to waver, but as he did so he raised his arms and launched a tremendous thunderbolt at them.

There was a noise so loud it was like a physical blow, and Kate found herself on her knees in the wet grass. Gordon was struggling to rise to his feet, David still at the water’s edge. Mr Flowerdew lay sprawled on his back.

Gordon reached him first.

“Are you hurt? What should I do?”

“Send Kate to fetch David so that we have a moment to talk.”

When he was sure she was out of earshot, he went on:

“I am dying, Gordon. What happened in the museum weakened me too much to withstand this.”

“No! There must be something. I’ll go and get help.”

He grasped Gordon's wrist with surprising strength even now. "There is nothing to be done. I have known all along that this would happen. It should have happened during the first battle here, all those years ago. Listen to me. You must look after the children. Take the car. Get them home. Then bring the car back and leave it here. Later, they will need to talk to you about everything; you are the only one who will understand now. With the rip in time healed, no one but us will remember what has happened tonight."

Kate arrived with an arm around David's shoulders, too stunned to speak.

He turned his head towards them. 'Thank you, both. No one else could have done what you did tonight. David, I know you have paid a terrible price. If there had been any other way..." He paused for breath, speaking now with more effort. "Go with Gordon now. You will not see me again. Accept what you hear about me."

"No," said Kate. "We won't leave you alone here. We'll get help."

He raised a hand and briefly touched her cheek. "Dear Kate. I have told Gordon already, I am dying. It is part of the price for our success. Truly, I don't mind. I have lived for a very long time.

"Go now. Goodbye. Thank you."

He closed his eyes.

Afterwards

Gordon pushed open the creaking gate and unlocked the front door. The hall was warmly welcoming after the December chill outside.

The big clock stared silently at him. He'd accepted now that no repairer would ever set it going again. It had died with John Flowerdew that night.

He was getting used to the idea of calling this place home, although the terms of the old man's will hadn't put it quite like that. A "life interest" he had, "holding it in trust until such time …" Such time as what, he still didn't know.

It was almost a week now since he'd seen the children. He sensed they were all drawing back from each other a little, trying to heal. No one else seemed to notice anything odd about them. Another part of John Flowerdew's legacy, he supposed.

To everyone else, he'd died of a heart attack; a good age, no need to mourn too much. His funeral had been well attended, for he'd had many friends. Two funerals he'd been to in that same week. Poor Andrew Nixon was the other one, murdered outside his house in Cramond by some madman with a sword, they said, and the police with no idea who'd done it.

When Gordon had been asked to go to the reading of John Flowerdew's will he'd been surprised, and when he'd understood why he was there, shocked out of speech for a while. Kate's mother and David's father had been there too, for there had been bequests for the children: a little money and a memento for each of them, he didn't know exactly what.

He'd weathered the inevitable comments and speculation at work; that was nothing, compared to what he'd been through.

It was still strange to go into the museum and find everything serene and normal: no shattered glass, no rumours of animals and no hint that such a thing as the Duddingston Hoard had ever existed. Another cache of relics filled the place in the round chamber, and the Ballachulish figure stood, as usual, in its cage of twigs.

He often looked at the clock, seeking a hint that he hadn't imagined everything, but the monkey stared ahead with inscrutable wooden eyes and gave no clue.

Kate drew her bedroom curtains, yawning. Tomorrow was Saturday, so if Ben didn't wake her by bursting into her bedroom there was a chance of a long lie. Not too long though: football practice to go to.

Just before she got into bed, she opened, as she always did now, the little box that used to hold Grandma Alice's gold necklace. Mum had been terribly angry at its loss for a while, but now it was as if she'd forgotten about it completely. Kate lifted out what the box held, and tilted it to catch the light. It was the little carved sea otter, the twin of the one in the museum. Mr Flowerdew had left it to her and when she held it, she felt somehow that he wasn't far away. Her memory of that dreadful night was being smoothed out a little as time went on, but she sometimes felt very old, not eleven at all.

She put the otter back in the little box and turned out the light.

"Bedtime, David."

"Okay. Hang on a minute. I'm just having some toast."

He brought the half-eaten slice through to the sitting room and flopped on to the sofa beside Alastair.

"Football tomorrow?"

"Yeah. Kate's coming round at half past nine."

Alastair looked up at the painting on the opposite wall.

"I wish I'd known him better. He obviously knew us."

David too was looking at it. It still made his heart ache every time he did.

The painting was his legacy from Mr Flowerdew. It showed David as he now was, and his dad, and Mum was with them, in her red fleece, happy and healthy and smiling. With them ... forever.

The Spanish Letters

Mollie Hunter

Can Jamie help Macey, the English spy, to thwart a Spanish plan to invade England and Scotland? Their perilous adventures take them through the streets and passageways of sixteenth-century Edinburgh to a breathtaking conclusion.

Mollie Hunter has a sure hand ...
The story has an indefinable atmosphere of Buchan in one of his more swashbuckling moods.
Times Literary Supplement

Quite outstanding.
Aberdeen Press and Journal

This thrilling tale of espionage set in Edinburgh in the year 1889 is as exciting as any modern 'spy' story.
Western Evening Herald

Kelpies

The Dark Shadow

Mary Rhind

Lizzie has been blind since she was very young. Full of hope she and her brother, Davie, embark on a journey to Edinburgh to seek a cure from the sacred water.

But their journey is filled with danger. It is the time of the Reformation in Scotland; churches are burning and people are fleeing for their lives.

The realization that the sinister leper who has followed their every movement is actually chasing them, quickly turns their excitement at their journey, into terror.

Winner of the BBC Scotland/ Scottish Library Association 'Quest for a Kelpie' Competition.

Blends an exciting tale of personal courage with the historical context of the Reformation in Scotland.
Scottish Children's Books

Kelpies